Dare to Love

Dare to Love

Portraits of Love
Book 2

Karen Rossi

A Karen Rossi Romance

Wisteria Publications

Wisteria Publications
507-4 Briar Hill Heights
New Tecumseth, ON
L9R 1Z7

Dare to Love
ISBN: 978-1-988763-10-1
Copyright © 2018 by Kaarina Brooks

Published in Canada 2018

Layout and Cover Art by Taria van Weesenbeek

Please contact the author at brooks.kaarina@gmail.com for any questions or comments.

Dedication

To my father who always said, "A woman should be full-figured, so a man has something to hold on to."

Other Books by Karen Rossi

"Portraits of Love" Series
    Dare to Dream
    Dare to Surrender
    Dare to Trust

No Home for My Heart
Despite Everything
Beyond Forgiveness

Acknowledgements

I want to thank Taria van Weesenbeek who has given so generously of her time to bring this novel to life.

Chapter One

Marita paused at the familiar studio door and drew in a few deep breaths. It wasn't just from having climbed up the long, steep stairwell that she found herself gasping for oxygen. The reason lay—or more than likely stood—behind the murky green door, where missing paint chips revealed a layer of brown under navy blue. A piece of paper taped to the door invited her to, "Walk in, please!"

She placed a hand on the worn brass doorknob, but couldn't make herself turn it.

"Coward," she cursed through clenched teeth. "Spineless jellyfish." But that helped about as much as all the self-cajoling she'd done in the bus on the way here. Okay, so it had got her this far, but now that the moment of truth was at hand, neither carrot nor stick could make her enter the studio and face the demon inside.

Demon? On the contrary. She'd been thinking about—more like dreaming about—the gorgeous man inside that studio for the last two months, ever since the spring session of art classes ended in June.

The squeaking door down at street level made

Marita turn. She looked down the stairwell at the two young women, squeezing in through the narrow door, both carrying bulky canvas bags. They stood for a moment, dismay painted on their faces, obviously weighing the challenge of climbing up the steep stairs.

"This house must have been designed by some evil architect," one of them muttered.

Marita watched them gather their belongings in preparation for the climb and suddenly panic seized her. She would look like a total dork if she stood there, blocking the way, while the women attempted to squeeze past her into the studio.

"Hey, could you please hold on a moment," Marita called down. "I forgot something in the car." And without debating her decision, she clacked down the stairs on her red heels, holding her large art bag in front of her.

She crowded past the women in the tiny landing and gave them a wide, apologetic smile. "Thanks for waiting. Those stairs aren't wide enough for more than one person at a time."

Especially when one of the said persons was more than slightly overweight. Like she, for instance.

Marita burst through the door into the warm, early September evening and hoisted the bag higher onto her shoulder. It contained her painting materials, but as far as she was concerned the brushes and paint tubes could be pitched into the nearest garbage container. There was no way she would ever take watercolour classes again. Not as long as Miguel Cordova was the teacher. No way, José!

But she had a momentary pang of regret, thinking of him upstairs in the studio. It would've been so gratifying just to see him again, after waiting for this moment for two long months.

They'd met only a couple of times last spring. Miguel had taken over the last two art classes when the regular teacher, Michael Merrick, had to leave town on business. And this handsome young artist with the dark, Spanish looks had made her forty-something heart beat like a pair of castanets. And every time he'd spoken to her, her insides had quaked like some silly teenager's, who had a crush on her middle-aged teacher.

Only this situation was more than slightly skewed in the opposite direction. She was a silly middle-aged student and he was a teenaged teacher—so to speak. He had to be at least ten years her junior. Maybe even more. He'd looked so young and smooth-cheeked, except for the heart-smashing shadow darkening his jaw by seven-thirty when the classes had started. With his aquiline nose, his brown doe-eyes with long dark lashes—the kind no human male should have been allowed to have—and his gleaming black hair combed smoothly back off his forehead, and that flat, almost concave stomach . . . Oh God, he was gorgeous with a capital G.

Marita stood on the sidewalk, staring stupidly at the brightly-lit corner window on the second floor. There he was. She almost dropped her art bag in excitement. His slim frame passed by the window . . . and was gone.

He wasn't very tall, she noted again. Which was okay, because she, herself, was barely five feet, so—

This was crazy. What did it matter what their height-ratio was? It would never be an issue in this life-time. But their weight-ratio was a matter of some amusement, because she knew she probably weighed more in her bra and panties than he did in a wet parka. This infatuation of hers was worse than crazy. It was insane.

Marita made her way slowly toward the bus stop. No way would she go to class and make an absolute fool of herself. If Miguel saw the stars in her eyes or— God forbid—saw her blush, he'd be surprised. Perhaps even amused. But certainly not flattered. A woman in her forties, for God's sake, acting like some love-sick high school kid. No way, José!

Marita still didn't know how she'd got through those two classes last spring. By exercising utmost self-control she'd managed to follow the lessons without drooling on her painting. At least not so anyone had noticed. She hoped.

If only Shaylee Palmer were coming with her to class now to boost her confidence. But her young friend was off with Michael Merrick, their art teacher, happily painting Europe in all the colours of love's rainbow that only the just-married could see. It was irony with a capital I that now Marita, in turn, was swooning over her art teacher. What was it about these artists that made their students fall head over heels for them? Besides their good looks, of course. Their sensitive, artistic hands? Or perhaps their ability to communicate with women so well in an easy-going manner? Probably all of the above. And more.

The bus arrived. Marita got on and with a few grunts she yanked the unruly art bag through the door. Why the hell hadn't she pitched the damned thing in the garbage bin by the bus stop?

"I am narrow where a woman should be narrow."
In front of the wide bathroom mirror Marita ran her

hands up and down her sides. Then she wiggled her ample bottom, barely covered by red bikini panties. "And I'm broad where a woman should be broad."

She stepped on the bathroom scales. Again.

Not obsessing. Just checking.

Damn. Up another pound. "Okay, dumpling," she spoke aloud at her reflection. "The scales do not lie. Time to bring out the diet shakes. Again."

She stepped off the scales and shook her wet, shaggy black hair. Then, batting her eyelashes, she leaned forward to make a comical moué at the mirror. But as her eyes went down to the full hips, she raised her upper lip in a snarl and turned away from the mirror in disgust.

So what if Ron had said he liked her hour-glass figure? He'd still left. Left for a woman with a washboard stomach and no hips. Showed he didn't mean a word of it. Ah, the mendacity of men.

On the way to the bedroom, Marita ran a five-finger comb through her wet mop and then gave her head another shake. The bed sheets received a cursory straightening, the pillow a quick plumping, and over the whole effort she threw a Mickey Mouse fleece. The pile of clothes from the chair went into a laundry basket in the closet, and in sixty seconds the bedroom was tidy.

Wearing a bright pink fleece bathrobe, Marita plodded into the kitchen in her fuzzy slippers and proceeded to pour cereal into a bowl.

"One hundred per cent Whole Grain. Very High Source of Fibre. Good Source of Eight Essential Nutrients," she read aloud from the back of the box. Sounded healthy enough. That couldn't be what was making her gain weight.

She opened the freezer door and reached for a bag of "World's Best Berries".

"All natural fruit. No sugar added. Source of fibre," she quoted. Also healthy. She shook a generous helping of blueberries on her cereal and sprinkled on a hefty dose of sugar from the ceramic bowl on the counter.

She got a quart of skim milk from the fridge. "Milk is an excellent source of Calcium and Vitamin D," she recited from the side of the carton. No one could say she didn't eat healthy foods. Okay, maybe the sugar, but surely that little bit couldn't make her this fat.

Marita carried her bowl into the dinette, connected to the small kitchen, and reached for the Sunday paper. After briefly scanning the headlines to ensure the world was still there, she flipped over to the comics, followed by her daily horoscope.

Taurus: "You are exuding a lovely charisma. You may find yourself inadvertently winning hearts and captivating minds. Follow your inclinations to greater happiness and fulfilment."

And which inclinations might they be? Now that she'd given up the art classes, she didn't have any other inclinations waiting to lead her to greater happiness and fulfilment. September was the month when she always—well, at least for the last three years since the divorce—gave her inclinations free rein by enrolling in as many evening classes as possible. They helped fill up the long, cold winter nights that would otherwise be spent in front of the tube. She'd tried everything from quilting to knitting, and from woodworking to watercolours. Watercolours? No more of that, thank you very much. Not while Miguel was the teacher.

"Good morning, Auntie Martha."

Marita turned and smiled at the young woman who shuffled into the dinette, stretching and yawning. Then she deliberately replaced the smile with a frown. "Lisa, darling, would you puh-leez stop calling me Auntie Martha."

Lisa grimaced, picked up the coffee carafe and filled the mug already waiting for her on the table.

"Sorry." She leaned over to top up Marita's mug. "I'm just so used to it." She squeezed around the table, and sat down by the wall. "I haven't seen you that often since you changed your name, you know."

"You've seen me often enough in the last two years. Plenty of time to get unused to the old name, my dear." Marita stirred a spoon of sugar into her coffee. "I'll bet your mother still refers to me as 'my older sister, Martha', doesn't she?"

Lisa grimaced her apology. "Fraid so. But I know you don't like that name and I am doing my best to remember. Mom always insists we shouldn't use nicknames for older . . . Whoops!" Lisa slapped a hand across her mouth. "Sorry, Auntie Marth . . . Whoops!"

"Whoops, whoops. That's not funny," Marita growled. She reached for a croissant. "And if this relationship of ours is to have any future at all, you're going to have to start remembering my name is now Marita Osborne. Not Martha Osmar." She placed the croissant firmly on the table and stood up to her full height. "Marita. Not Martha," she pronounced. "Martha was a poor, downtrodden housewife, only loved for her culinary skills. Marita is a witty, self-reliant, vibrant woman who will not give the time of day to any man, unless he loves her for her witty, self-reliant and vibrant, albeit amplitudenous self."

Or that's how the script was supposed to read, anyway.

Lisa clapped enthusiastically. "Hoo-ray, Auntie Marita! Even if I've never heard the word amplitudenous before, it sounds totally impressive."

"And no more 'Auntie' either, if you don't mind. Makes me sound old. I'm Marita." She sat down again. "And I'll thank you to remember that, my dearest and only niece."

"Yes, Marita," Lisa bowed her head obediently, but her blue eyes sparkled with laughter. "But you'll have to give me some time to get used to the idea. No fair booting me out of the apartment after just a couple of days."

"All right. A few days it will be." Marita pushed the newspaper toward Lisa and pointed to an ad with her red manicured fingernail. "In fact, I'll give you till we move into our new digs next Saturday."

Lisa grabbed the paper. "Oh, great! Is this the new apartment, Aun—Marita?"

"Yes, that's what your Aun-Marita has rented. I'll give them a call right after breakfast to confirm it's empty and clean. The good thing is, it's not too far from your college."

The lazy Saturday morning was interrupted by Marita's phone lying on the stove. Lisa bounced up to answer it.

Rolling her eyes dramatically she handed the phone to Marita and mouthed the words, "A man".

Marita frowned. Surely not Ron again. "Yes?" she said rather sharply, but the next moment her face flared up with flaming heat and quickly she turned away from Lisa's curious eyes.

"Oh . . . hi, Miguel." She covered the receiver and

took a deep breath. "I'm fine. How're you?"

Discreetly Lisa withdrew into the living room, but Marita guessed she'd probably detected the wobble in her voice.

"I was worried when you didn't show up Tuesday night for class," Miguel's deep voice said into her ear, making her skin quiver with pleasure. "I hope nothing's wrong?"

"No, no. Nothing's wrong. I just decided since my paintings are never going to hang in the Louvre, why waste my time and yours. Better you concentrate on those students who can actually paint. And I can spend my money on stuff I can benefit from." She blabbered on, unable to stop herself. "Like yoga classes, or salsa dancing, or tennis, or something." She gave a short, low laugh that failed to sound funny, but succeeded in covering her agitation. "I only made up my mind yesterday, and didn't have time to call you. Sorry."

"That's okay. You don't owe me any explanations. I just called because . . ." There was a pause.

Was he trying to think of an excuse why he called? Nonsense. He just didn't like losing a paying client. But immediately Marita chastised herself for this mean-spirited thought. Miguel wasn't like that.

"I only took the spring session class to fill my lonely evenings," she explained and heaved a loud, dramatic sigh.

"So did I hear you say you're going to take up salsa dancing instead?"

"I might." Not bloody likely. Salsa was like exercising, which was akin to visiting a dentist.

"Going with your boyfriend?"

Not for a second did Marita think he asked that in

order to find out whether she actually had a boyfriend. Well, maybe for one hopeful second she did. But why on earth should he give a damn?

"With my boyfriend? No. With my niece. She arrived a couple of days ago to live with me and I thought it might be good for her to take up some physical activities to balance her studies." When had she learned to lie so smoothly? "She's starting a course next week at the Wilfred Brown Community College downtown."

"Okay. But I still wish you'd come to art class. It was fun with you there last June. I've missed you."

Marita's breath rushed into her lungs in a surprised whoosh. Miguel had missed her? Her? Fat chance. The pun made her cough out a burst of dry laughter.

"You're kidding! With all those lovely ladies surrounding you, how could you possibly miss me? I assume all the Sues and Paulines and Britneys have returned to class this fall?"

"Yes, they've all returned," he said. "Every last one of them." He sounded strangely dismissive.

"And?"

"And they're exactly the same as last spring."

Marita couldn't believe her ears. He sounded thoroughly fed up with all those beautiful, sex-starved women. But how in God's name could Miguel not appreciate them? They had buzzed around the previous teacher, Michael, and had given her friend, Shaylee, such a hard time. Of course Michael had encouraged their fawning until he fell for Shaylee, but surely Miguel, a single man, would take advantage of the situation. Like, why wouldn't he?

"Your girlfriend disapproves of them?" Marita asked and then wanted to kick herself. Could her fishing be more obvious?

Miguel laughed. "No. I'm just not into that particular type of woman."

Marita wanted to ask what particular type of women he was into, but she knew the answer for sure would not be, "middle-aged, short dumplings."

Instead she said, "Well, I'm afraid you'll have to get along without my amusing presence, because I definitely won't be coming to art class this fall. Besides, my niece and I are moving into a bigger apartment next weekend and it's even farther from the art classes. Lisa needs a bedroom. She can sleep on the living room couch for only so long. It's not even a pull-out."

The sound of his deep laughter spread over her like a satin shawl. "Poor girl," Miguel said. And then he dropped a bombshell. "Listen, if you need help with your move, don't hesitate to call me."

Marita gulped. Miguel was offering to help the move? But he wasn't even very muscular. His incredibly beautiful, lithe and perfect body was easier to envision in bullfighter's tights than in mover's coveralls.

"Hey, that's awfully nice of you, but you're not—"

"I said if you need me. Don't feel you have to." He sounded slightly offended. Because she didn't immediately rush to thank him? Or had he somehow read her thoughts—that she doubted his strength?

"Thanks, I'll call you," she stammered.

"Sure you won't change your mind about the art classes?" His plaintive tone almost made her relent.

"Well, maybe next year." Or whenever she was over this totally ridiculous schoolgirl crush on him. She refused to glorify it by calling it love. Or even infatuation. It was pure, one hundred per cent idiocy.

After she hung up, Marita briskly picked up the paper.

"I'll give the landlord a ring right now and start this day rolling," she called to Lisa.

Activity was a sure cure for everything. Even for feeling like crap when a husband leaves you for a younger, more beautiful woman with firm arms and a tight butt. Calling Hillary a "Bimbo" would've sounded like she was spiteful and jealous, which she wasn't. Except maybe about the younger, more beautiful part. And maybe the firm arms and tight butt.

And activity was also a cure for feeling like a dork when you fell for a younger man. Especially one who almost looked like a teen-ager. Now, if only she were a size zero and a half . . .

And if wishes were horses.

Lisa came and sat at the table again. Of course she'd heard every word Marita had spoken. "Who was that man with the lovely, deep, voice?"

"My art teacher from last spring," Marita replied as nonchalantly as she could. "Miguel Cordova. He took over the last two classes when the regular teacher, Michael Merrick, had to go to Montréal to look after an art project. A mural or some such thing. Now Miguel is teaching the class full time because Michael has gone to Europe for a year-long honeymoon with his wife."

"So why was he calling you? Or shouldn't I ask?"

"You shouldn't ask. But I'll tell you anyway. He was wondering why I didn't come to the first class. I had registered for it but, as you heard me telling him, it would be silly to start a class when we'll be moving. It would be too inconvenient to get to it." The fact that she was an infatuated coward would never be revealed to anyone. No way, José!

"You didn't go because you're moving to a bigger apartment to accommodate me." Lisa reached over to give Marita a kiss on the cheek. "I really appreciate that, but I feel bad."

"Please don't, because this isn't about you, young lady. I've been looking for something bigger since I got my promotion a couple of months ago." She blew on her fingers and rubbed them on her ample bosom. "I'm now in charge of organizing all the menus for the biggest events, so I get to work with the catering company's VIP clients. I even have a few people working under me, so it's time to move to a place that suits my new station in life."

When her sister, Rosalyn, had called and asked if Lisa could come and stay with her for the fall and spring semesters, it had been the impetus she'd needed. Of course the pay raise would be quickly eaten up by the higher rent, but Lisa's room and board would more than make up for it.

"A newer apartment with a kitchen that's big enough for a dishwasher. I mean, can you think of a better reason to move?"

Lisa laughed. "I totally agree. After two days of washing dishes by hand I'm convinced a dishwasher is a necessity and not a luxury."

"You bet. And the place has an elevator." Marita breathed in dreamy ecstasy and raised her hand slowly, palm up. "Living on the fourth floor of an ancient walk-up isn't an option any more for someone of my advanced age." She knew she probably would come to miss the forced exercise the stairs provided, since going to a gym was definitely not on her radar screen. "Just think what I've been going through for three years."

Lisa snorted. "Auntie Martha, you're not old. And you're in great shape."

"Well, if you'd stop calling me Auntie Martha it would help me feel about ten years younger."

"Sorry, Marita. I'm working on it. Honest, I am," Lisa poured herself another cup of coffee. "But aren't you going to miss the art lessons?"

"Look, I only took the lessons last spring for something to do." When Ron left she had not only lost a husband, but a whole circle of friends. All couples. But Lisa didn't need to know that. It would only produce those maudlin, sympathetic noises she'd heard enough of, thank you very much. "I've no more talent for art than does a chair leg. Maybe even less. Look around you. Do you see any paintings hanging on the walls with my name on them?"

"No. But I thought you just never got around to hanging them up."

Marita didn't have the heart to mock this sincere show of faith by bursting into a loud guffaw. Instead she said, "There was nothing worth hanging up, believe me."

She stood up and picked up the apartment ad. "Now I'm going to make this phone call, so stop distracting me with your comments."

Lisa reached for an oatmeal biscuit from the open cookie tin on the table. "Okay. But what about this yoga you mentioned on the phone? Or salsa dancing? Are you really going to take up something like that after we move?"

"Definitely not." Marita dialed the number. "I'm not into twisting my body into unnatural shapes."

"But salsa dancing would be fun and good for you." Lisa closed the lid of the cookie tin. "I'll go with you, if you want. I've always thought it might be fun to learn salsa, but those classes weren't offered at home."

"Thanks, but I'll choose skipping instead," Marita said as she listened for the ringtone.

"Skipping?" Lisa frowned. "With a rope?"

"No, skipping. As in skipping yoga and skipping salsa and skipping all other forms of sweat-producing activity. Now, please let me make this call without another interruption."

Lisa moved off into the living room and flopped down on the couch that still had her bedding spread out on it.

A few minutes later Marita joined her and announced, "We're in luck. The apartment's vacant and clean. I can pick up the key any time. You want to come and take a look at your future home and help me decide where to place the furniture? We'll have to take a couple of buses to get there, but we've got all day."

Funny how busy she always used to be before Ron left. Dinner parties to prepare for friends. Dinner parties at friends' homes. And sniffing the lovely perfume—not hers—on Ron's shirts. And soon after that she'd stopped being so busy.

Chapter Two

Marita closed a big plastic bag containing linens with a tie-on and heaved it beside several other bags lined up against the bedroom wall. The apartment was beginning to look like a tornado had passed through it.

"Do you think I should call Miguel to help with the move on Saturday?" she called to Lisa. "He offered."

"Why not? We can always use an extra pair of hands at the new place to move stuff around." Lisa carried a box stuffed with shoes into the hall. "Some of these suckers are pretty heavy."

"We better keep that tiny entrance hall clear for the movers," Marita said. "Let's store everything in the living room for now. This narrow hall is another thing I'm not going to miss."

"Too bad you couldn't stay in the house where you and Uncle Ron lived," Lisa said. "I loved it. It was so roomy and beautiful."

"Yes, it was. But I couldn't afford to buy him out." The money from the house sale had provided her with a nest egg until she'd found a job with a catering company that appreciated her culinary skills. It seemed Ron's finances hadn't been as solid as he'd let on, or then he was very clever at hiding his assets, so there wasn't much left for her after the dust settled. "Water under the bridge. I don't even think about it any more."

Not much. If only she had a profession to fall back on she'd be living pretty. But over the seventeen years of marriage the only thing that all that cooking and entertaining had produced were twenty extra pounds. Which was something Ron had never got tired of commenting about.

"An old, fat, unappealing wife," he had confided to a friend as his reason for shifting to a younger, slimmer, more appealing model. And of course this friend had kindly passed this flattering bit of information to Marita. Ouch! Water under the bridge? More like Chinese water torture that never stopped gnawing at her. Not Ron's leaving, of course, but his hurtful words.

Marita passed the full-length hall mirror that hadn't been taken down yet. Old, fat and unappealing. Was she really? She stopped briefly and then turned away with a grimace. Yep, Ron was right. But who cared, anyhow?

"So should I call Miguel?" she asked again. Once upon a time her social circle, hers and Ron's, had contained lots of friends whom she could have called on for help with the move. The occasion would have been turned into a fun social evening of light unpacking, drinking and eating. That, too, was water under the bridge.

"Yes." Smartly Lisa handed her the phone from the kitchen counter.

Marita almost took it, but then let her arm drop.

"Hey, why don't you call him?" she asked brightly, as though this clever idea had just popped into her head.

"Me?" Lisa squealed. "Why on earth should I call him? I don't even know the guy."

"Tell him I'm too busy to talk, but that we could use his help." Oh, brother. What a pile of crap. And what would Miguel think? "Well, it's true," she added, when Lisa's eyebrows shot up in a you-gotta-be-kidding look. "I'm totally over-encumbered."

"Over-encumbered? Marita, get real. Here's the phone." Lisa took Marita's hand into hers and firmly placed the phone into it. "Call this Miguel guy and tell him you appreciate his kind offer of help and would like to take him up on it."

Attempting to look nonchalant, Marita shrugged and turned away from Lisa's puzzled eyes. "Thank you, Lisa, for scripting my phone call. I'm sure I couldn't do it without you."

But when Miguel answered, Marita was relieved to have the script all ready because it was true. She couldn't have done it on her own without stammering and blushing.

Leaning against the balcony railing, Marita surveyed her new domain. Seven floors below sparkled the outdoor swimming pool surrounded by shrubs and beds of fall flowers but minus the swimmers. Yes, flowers would be the first thing she would buy for her balcony in the spring. Potted geraniums, plus a couple of plastic chairs and a little table to hold a glass of wine while she read her book and listened to the water splashing in the pool and saw it glimmering through the glassed-in balcony.

She returned into the living room and spread out

her arms. What a beautiful place she had, if she ignored the total mayhem surrounding her. The movers had brought everything in and had carried the furniture into the appropriate rooms. Now it was a matter of unpacking all the bags and boxes that lay scattered along the walls.

"This is heaven," she breathed. "I couldn't be happier. Two bedrooms, two bathrooms, a real kitchen with a dishwasher and a breakfast table. Not to mention a balcony. But I'll mention it anyway. A balcony."

Lisa laughed. "If this is heaven, think what it'll it be like when it's all organized and neat."

"It'll be paradise. There's nothing more I could want in life." She dropped down on her knees in front of a large cardboard box and eagerly tore at the flaps to discover what it had swallowed.

"Nothing?" Lisa smiled mischievously. "How about a man?" She placed the glass vase she'd just unwrapped onto the kitchen counter, among candle holders, trivets, and other paraphernalia.

Marita snorted. "Man. Schman. Totally over-rated. Who needs 'em?"

"I hope you do, because you asked me to come and help."

At the sound of the deep male voice, Marita whirled around on her knees to see Miguel standing at the door that had been left ajar for him. He held out a bouquet of flowers and bowed. "For your new home, milady."

Marita took him in with one quick glance. No man had a right to be so beautiful. If anything, the deep summer tan glowing on his face made him even more handsome than he'd been when she last saw him at the end of June. He obviously hadn't shaved this morning and the dark stubble on his chin made him look dangerously alluring.

"Oh, darn, you're too late. Everything's in place already." She hoped her voice sounded bright and funny. "Well, thanks for coming, anyway. Bye."

She grinned as she got up from the floor, hoping she executed the move reasonably gracefully, and walked toward him with legs she willed not to wobble. "How are you, Miguel?"

It was now necessary to shake his hand. After all, they hadn't seen each other for two months. Surely she could do that without her legs buckling under her.

But when she got near him, Miguel put the bouquet on a nearby box and, stepping forward, he took her in his arms.

"It's great to see you again, Marita," he said and then he did the unthinkable. He kissed her. Not on the cheek like a friend, nor on two cheeks like a European, but right on the mouth. And it wasn't only a stiff-lipped peck either, but a hundred dollar kiss with soft lips, suction and the works.

Too soon he raised his head, and when he looked at Marita with his dark brown eyes the room tilted dangerously. She had time to pray he wouldn't release her until her balance returned, while simultaneously offering up another prayer that he would never release her.

When the air returned into her lungs she said, "Great to see you, Miguel." And somehow she made it sound like the kiss had been the most natural greeting in the world, instead of a tsunami-producing earthquake.

"Great to see you, too, Marita." He picked up the

flowers and handed them to her. "For your new home. I hope you've unearthed some container to put them in."

Marita took the bouquet and buried her fiery face in the equally red carnations. "Beautiful," she breathed.

She turned to face Lisa's open-mouthed stare. "This is my niece, Lisa," she told Miguel. "I told you she's staying with me while she attends Wilfred Brown College. Lisa, this is my art teacher. Well, I guess I should say my former art teacher. But he would have been my art teacher if I—" Marita realized she was blabbering and stopped. "Miguel Cordova. Lisa Howe."

She noted a flash of interest in Lisa's pretty blue eyes, and the smile Miguel directed at Lisa was a killer. Lisa was young and very pretty. What man wouldn't smile at her like that?

But did Miguel have to?

Oh God, what was she thinking? Marita stuffed the little green monster deep down inside her and, feeling like a yenta introducing two young people to each other, she smiled benevolently at them. They looked so cute together. She took the vase Lisa handed her and went to fill it with water.

"Miguel, you're just in time," she called brightly from the kitchen. Too brightly? "A minute ago I located the wine bottles in a box where I'd also cleverly stashed some plastic wine glasses."

"But I haven't done any work yet," Miguel protested.

"Oh, but you will." She arranged the flowers into the vase and set it on a brand new round breakfast table with the packing slip still attached. The kitchen was the only room where it was possible to sit down. On four brand new wooden chairs, no less.

With a flourish Marita pulled out a chair for Miguel. "You can be the first to use my new kitchen furniture. If you please, monsieur. I hope you like red?"

Miguel turned the chair around and sat down legs splayed. He leaned his dark chin on his fists on the back of the chair. "Red's great," he said. "Did you also happen to cleverly stash the bottle opener in the same box?"

"*Mais oui.*" Marita brandished the cork screw and busied herself with opening the bottle, refusing to look down at those fabulous thighs in the well-fitting jeans. Maybe he was slim and not too tall, but he sure was an extremely well-put-together package.

Lisa gave some plastic glasses a wipe with a paper towel and set them on the table. "These'll have to do, I guess, until Marita locates her crystal goblets."

Marita snorted. "That'll be one helluva long wait." She pulled the cork, poured the wine and seated herself. The small table didn't allow for great distances between chairs, and sure enough, his bare arm came into contact with hers quite inadvertently. It remained there, setting off another tsunami inside her.

"Do you know, Miguel, Marita thinks she's in paradise?" Lisa revealed.

Miguel raised his glass. "Here's to your paradise, Marita. May it always be cosy and comfortable."

"Like it is now," Marita crowed. "But seriously, it's got everything I need. And it'll be great once everything's in place and my favourite kitten on black velvet is hung on the wall." Of course she had to say that to deliberately shock the professional artist sitting beside her. He already knew she had no talent in art, but why on earth did she have to make him think she was completely unsophisticated as far as art was concerned?

"Kitten on black velvet?" Miguel said with a straight face. "Now, that's interesting. Do you also happen to have some paint-by-number pieces?"

"A few. My taste in art runs from Michelangelo to Mickey Mouse." She took a sip of wine, adding more liquid to the rolling surf inside her.

"Wow! I'm impressed." His mouth spread into a wide grin that revealed a row of white even teeth.

"Marita's being silly," Lisa put in. "She knows about art. She's a very good painter."

"I know. I've seen her . . . efforts." Kindly Miguel didn't expand on that.

"But you should've seen the paintings in the house she and Uncle Ron used to own before they div—" Lisa began eagerly and broke off as Marita's eyebrows drew together in disapproval.

"Well," Lisa finished lamely. "You are the one who made the house cosy and comfortable, Auntie Martha." Aghast, she slapped a hand on her mouth. "Oh my God! I'm sorry."

Marita's breath exploded in an exasperated puff. "My secret is out." Although she was annoyed, she patted Lisa's hand. "It's all right, dearie, I'll forgive you this once. But next time you slip, it's off with your head."

She turned to Miguel. "Yes, it is true. My name used to be Martha. But I'm a born-again divorcée with a new name, a new life, and now a new apartment. And don't you believe a word she said. That house was much too big to be cosy and comfortable. This apartment is more my style."

She was thankful Miguel was sensitive enough not to pursue the subject.

"I think this apartment's great, Marita." He set his glass on the table and got up. "So, let's get this show on the road. What can I do?"

Lisa also stood up, looking relieved she was still alive after her blunder. "Why don't Miguel and I unpack the boxes while Marita puts the things where she wants them to go."

"Sounds like a plan," Marita agreed.

Actually she would have preferred for Miguel to remain standing there, like a handsome Greek statue, while she and Lisa unpacked. It felt good—too good—to have him here, now that she was over the shock of seeing him again, and had calmed down somewhat from his unexpectedly friendly greeting.

She watched as he effortlessly picked up a box and placed it on the table. His bare arms were sinewy, though not bulging with muscles, and she didn't need to be reminded how strong they were, as they'd firmly held her against him only a few heartbeats ago. Oh, how good it had felt to be held and kissed by him.

"Hey, Earth to Marita," Lisa called. "Stop dreaming and start putting the dishes away. Soon we're going to have to put them on the floor."

Marita picked up a few plates and turned to hide her burning cheeks. When she felt it was safe to face the others, she said, "You two are such a great unwrapping team, I can't keep up with you."

And Miguel and Lisa did look like they would make a good team in any situation. They reached into the box, and as they dug for articles his dark head almost touched her blond one. And from the quick laughter, when they both happened to reach for the same dish, Marita could tell an easy camaraderie was settling between them.

She struggled to keep her mind on the cups and plates but failed. Maybe they would start dating. Miguel had seemed to indicate he didn't have a girlfriend and Lisa didn't know anybody in Toronto yet. What could be more natural? The two were probably as close in age as she and Miguel were, but their age difference was in the direction sanctioned by society. Marita would be considered a cougar if she ever aspired to have a relationship with him. A cougar? What a horrible word!

As the morning wore on and the boxes and bags slowly emptied, this word wasn't something Marita wanted to carry around in her head, but it refused to leave her. Cougar. But, hey, who said anything about aspiring to have a relationship with Miguel, anyway? Certainly not her.

This was stupid. There was only one thing to do. Kick the idea right out in the open. Expose it to the bright light of day.

"Hey," she said brightly. "How about let's take a break and you two go get us some lunch? My treat, of course."

She gave her back a rub. It wasn't aching, but older people always did that, didn't they? And she was the old person in the room. "You deserve more than take-out pizza, but I can't imagine getting all dolled up to go to a restaurant."

Miguel placed a saucepan on the table. "Please, let me get the lunch as my treat to welcome you into your new home."

"I accept," Marita said. "But only because that will allow you to feel noble." She reached for a brochure in a pile of papers on the counter. "The pizza place around the corner was cunning enough to leave their ad in my mailbox. With directions."

Lisa brushed off her jeans. "You call them, Marita, and we'll head over."

Smiling took more effort than the whole morning of unpacking, but Marita managed. "Yes. You two youngsters go fetch the pizza while I rest my weary old bones." God, did she have to slather it on that thick? What an idiot. But it did get a laugh out of them all.

When Miguel and Lisa were gone, Marita brushed a hand across the smooth, polished surface of the table and then set out three plates. Was she really feeling jealous of her niece? That was stupendously stupid. She would have to get over it immediately because when—not if—Miguel and Lisa started dating, she would see them together all the time when he came to pick her up. And Lisa would talk about him constantly, telling Marita intimate details about their latest date. That would be pretty hard to take unless she managed to get a stranglehold on the green monster inside her and snuff the beast right out of existence. Right now!

Only a few hours ago, standing on her balcony, she'd felt like she'd died and gone to heaven. And when Miguel had kissed her— Wow! It had transported her head first into paradise.

But that particular paradise wasn't for her. It was waiting there for Lisa. And as a nice auntie, she ought to have been ecstatic her niece had found someone as great as Miguel so soon after moving into the city.

She had absolutely no reason to feel jealous. But she was. Maybe she should write a letter to a love columnist.

Dear Abby, I am jealous of my niece who is dating the man I am crazy about. He is at least ten years my junior and doesn't know I have these feelings for him. What should I do? Signed, Fat Aunt.

Dear Fat Aunt, Get over it. Find someone your own age and leave the youngsters alone. Signed, Abby.

Good advice, Abby. Thank you.

Marita ripped off three sheets of paper towel for napkins, folded them and placed them beside each plate. Surely she could find someone more suitable—which of course meant older—to occupy her dreams. There were plenty of middle-aged men in Toronto.

She poured out the wine into three glasses of stemware that she had just unearthed. Yeah, sure there were lots of middle-aged men, but were they looking for middle-aged women? Not bloody likely. They were all after younger, sexier women who would give their flagging libidos a boost. With a bit of help from a little pill, if necessary.

Men like Ron.

Lisa was laughing at some joke when she and Miguel walked in. He placed the large pizza box on the counter and Lisa doled out the slices.

"Looks good enough to eat," Marita said, rolling her eyes with mock greed as they all sat down.

Miguel raised his wine glass. "Another toast to Marita's new home. This time with real wine glasses." His smile was wide and his teeth flashed white. Marita had the urge to reach across the table and stroke his unshaven chin. Mentally she slapped her hand. Lecherous old lady. Cougar.

Instead she joined Lisa's "Yea!" She clinked glasses with them, confident that her performance was superb. "I had to find the real wine glasses because clacking with plastic just didn't sound right."

Lisa got up to get a second slice of pizza. "So,

Marita, are you really going to join a salsa dance class?"

Marita frowned. Why was Lisa bringing that up now? Hadn't they already been through the whole scenario? It wasn't something she wanted to discuss in front of Miguel, anyway, because it brought attention to the twenty extra pounds she carried around, mostly on her hips. Okay, boobs, too, but they could be considered an asset, unlike her ass. She smiled at the clever mental pun, which her niece took as a sign of consent.

"Yeah, I think it's a great idea. I'm all for going," Lisa enthused.

Miguel nodded. "You're right, it's a great pastime. In fact, I was telling Lisa I've been going to salsa evenings for several years."

Now, wouldn't you know she would accidentally stumble upon an activity he was good at? First art, now salsa. Or maybe it wasn't an accident. Marita couldn't recall, but perhaps last spring at one of the art classes the subject of salsa may have come up. It sure was easy to imagine him dancing a hot number. Marita could already feel his strong, sinewy arms around her, the way they'd felt earlier today.

"It'll be good for both of you," Miguel went on. "Meet new people. Get some exercise. And have fun doing it."

Of course he wouldn't come right out and say it, but the implication was definitely there: it was good for her because she was fat and badly in need of exercise. But he was right, of course. Didn't the bathroom scales confirm that fact each and every morning?

Lisa's eyes sparkled. "So Marita, it's settled. I'll look up the nearest class."

Marita gave Lisa's hand a pat. A lovely, elderly

touch. "Oh, okay, then," she said. "If you're too timid to go by yourself, I'll come with you to a couple of classes."

Miguel nodded. "You'll enjoy the dancing, I know."

Marita gave a short laugh. "No way, José. I'll just be watching. My ex and I took ballroom dancing years ago, but I never exactly morphed into Ginger Rogers." That was a years before Ron decided to dance off with another partner.

"So you know the tango? That's great," Miguel got up and extended an arm to Marita with an exaggerated bow. "Madame, may I?"

Marita flushed bright red and knew the others couldn't have missed seeing it. "Don't be silly, my boy," she cried. "There's not even any music."

"We'll make our own music." And Miguel began to hum a very energetic rendition of "Kiss of Fire" as he pulled Marita up onto her feet.

There was nothing to do but submit, because refusing and making a scene would have been embarrassing. With his arm firmly around her waist he drew her to the middle of the living room floor, which now was almost free of boxes. Marita's heart took up the flaming rhythm of the tango, only the pulsing inside her was ten times faster and the heat easily equalled the fiery kiss in the song.

"You dance like an angel," Miguel whispered in her ear. "Light and easy."

Marita felt the arm around her waist tighten a notch and his dark head inched closer to hers. His face was slightly above hers, and when he leaned down to place his cheek against hers, she stopped breathing.

Whenever she'd stepped on Ron's toes at the dance classes he'd let the whole room know about it. He kept insisting it was her fault, though his toes were always the ones that were in the wrong place. But now there seemed to be no such issues and her feet easily found their place.

At one point Miguel's knee found its way between her thighs, sending flames coursing up through her body. Her eyes closed in ecstasy, and for a brief moment she abandoned herself to the sweet sensations that thrummed inside her.

Suddenly her eyes popped open. She realized Miguel had stopped humming and they were standing, his arm still holding her against the length of his hard body. She had to remind herself to breathe.

He rested his forehead against hers. "You're perfect," he said. "You'll be dipping and swirling in salsa class in no time."

With supreme effort, while every nerve of her body screamed in protest, Marita shrugged herself away from him. "Dipping and swirling, eh? Sounds like a cooking class to me," she remarked airily and went to get another slice of pizza. Which she wanted about as much as a piece of uncooked liver. Her whole body trembled, and she remained with her back to him until she had calmed down—at least on the outside.

This was insane. The man had to get out of her life and never return. Now. Immediately. Before her heart and even her logical mind were irrevocably lost. Go away, young man.

"Listen, speaking of cooking, I would like to take you for dinner tonight," Miguel said out of the blue, with a total disregard for her thoughts. Didn't the man realize he was being dismissed from her life? Kicked out forever. Exiled. Or more like exorcised. Didn't he understand she didn't want him messing up her head?

Because she wanted him—so desperately wanted him—but didn't want him in her life.

Or whatever. Already her thoughts were crazy, mixed-up nonsense.

She sat down and concentrated on cutting up her pizza.

"I was thinking that with everything not in place yet, eating out tonight would be the logical thing to do," Miguel explained as he helped himself to another slice. "Will you come?"

Marita told herself she had no way of knowing if the invitation was in the plural or the singular. Or if it was directed at her or Lisa. She hesitated so long before replying that her slice of pizza started to resemble ground beef.

"Marita, what do you say?" Lisa touched her wrist lightly.

Marita's head jerked up. "I'm sorry. About . . .?" How obtuse could she pretend to be without appearing like a total idiot? But she had to play for time. An answer was required. Now.

"Miguel asked if we'd come for dinner. Didn't you hear?"

"I'm sorry. I though he was speaking to you."

"No, I was asking you both," Miguel said.

"Then you should have said 'youse' to be clear," Marita instructed him.

As she'd intended, that got a laugh out of them. Marita even managed to make her own chuckle sound realistic, though she didn't feel the least bit humorous.

"Sure, I'll come along as your chaperone," she said and didn't even look up to see how Miguel took this asinine statement.

"Marita's always joking about her age," Lisa said,

shaking her head. "She's not as old as she pretends to be."

"I'm not even as funny as I pretend to be," Marita added with a grimace. "A total phony." That elicited another laugh, but Miguel had no way of knowing she meant every syllable.

"You're the most real and honest woman I've met in a long while," Miguel said. He looked at Marita and his sincere, dark brown eyes burned into hers.

Marita reeled. She had to lower her gaze before this onslaught. The man really had a talent for shocking her today. First he kissed her hello. Then he danced a hot tango with her. And now this flattery. Flattery, that's all it was.

"Oh, you're probably talking about the natural colour of my nails," she said and spread out her fingers that glowed with bright red nail polish.

"They're very pretty," Miguel said and lightly brushed his hand over them. "I like them."

He was doing it again. The man was incredible.

"Does anyone want more pizza or shall I put the rest in the fridge?" Marita asked, rising. She needed time to bring the roiling emotions inside her down to a tropical storm.

Miguel put down his napkin and got up from the table. "Not me, thanks. Better get on with the job." With ease he picked up a large box from the floor and placed it on a chair for easier emptying. "Let's see what this one's hiding."

The phone rang in the living room and Lisa hurried to answer. Marita could hear her talking, and overheard the word, "Mommy".

"Sounds like my sister, Rosalyn. Lisa's mother," she told Miguel. "Checking to see how her daughter is settling in, no doubt."

Her only sister had been her main source of emotional support when she'd gone through rough times with Ron. Their mother lived too far away to have been much comfort to her except by telephone.

Lisa returned shortly. "Mom's coming over later tonight to see the place."

Marita grimaced. "I knew it. And Rosalyn will tell me exactly where I should have placed each piece of furniture. Of course, as the artistic one in the family, she thinks it's perfectly okay to throw around her opinions." She grinned, putting an arm around Lisa's shoulders. "Just kidding. But I'll bet she won't be able to resist at least one correction."

"Marita's right, you know," Lisa said with a good-humored chuckle. "My Mom really is like that."

"But only because she's got such a good eye for decorating," Marita admitted. She walked over to a brand new armchair and gave it a shove. "I think I'd better get the living room in shape so she'll have a comfy place to sit and sip her wine."

"You're very thoughtful of others," Miguel said, making Marita's heart start the wild tango again.

"And thou art too kind, sir." She made a clowning courtly bow.

"Art?" Lisa exclaimed. "Very clever, Marita. Talking to an art teacher."

"No pun intended," Marita confessed. "It was only a fortunate accident."

Miguel grinned. "You see? My opinion is spot on."

"About what?" Marita asked. "That I have accidents?"

"That you're honest and sincere."

"Oh, pshaw! You make me blush." She wished he

wouldn't keep insisting on that. If he only knew she was the biggest phony in town pretending she wanted him to be interested in Lisa, while hungrily hankering after him herself.

Cougar.

Chapter Three

By late afternoon the apartment had taken on an organized and comfortable appearance.

Miguel nodded his approval. "I like it." He had taken the last of the empty boxes down to the recycling area in the basement. "It's very cosy."

"Nice and comfy," Lisa agreed.

Marita surveyed her home with a deep sense of pride. Yes, it did look more like her paradise now. There were off-white sheers on the floor-to-ceiling living room window, and on the coffee table sat the flowers Miguel had brought. The sofa and armchairs were an intimate wine red, and the homespun, off-white area rug provided warmth to the dark hardwood floors. Evening was falling and a small lamp on a side table gave a soft, rosy glow. The whole room was an oasis of peace and calm.

"It's not modern decor, that's for sure," Marita said. "But I didn't want that. I don't think my old pieces of furniture from back home would've felt comfortable in a totally modern steel and glass setting. I was afraid my great-grandma's rocking chair wouldn't fit in here because of the long runners, but I think it looks very content there in the corner. As a kid I got such a thrill rocking in it."

"It looks interesting," Miguel said. "Mind if I try it?" He sat in the antique rocker, painted shiny white, and immediately it swung back, catching him off guard. He grabbed the armrests and put his feet on the floor to stop the motion, laughing in surprise. "Whoa! This really gives a good ride."

If only there were some way to can that deep, masculine laughter so Marita could listen to it when alone. The sound made giggles bubble up from inside her and she laughed with him. "I know. When I was little I was afraid to lean back on it, because I thought it would fall over."

"I'm not little, but I sure felt the same way," Miguel said and got up.

"But when I was older I rocked it pretty wildly," Marita bragged.

"A wild woman, eh?" Miguel said with the hint of a salacious smile, and came toward her with a slight, suggestive swagger.

Marita backed off, palms upraised. "Not at all. I knew the rocker was never in danger of falling."

"And you?" Miguel asked, stopping too close for comfort.

Marita gulped. It sure sounded like he was fishing for information about her status. How could she give a comical comeback to that question? Was she in danger of falling? Hell, she'd already toppled right over!

"Me? I'm too wise ever to fall." To hide her confusion and to get off this topic, she turned to Lisa and asked, "So, will you get all dolled up for when Miguel picks us up for dinner?"

"Oh!" Lisa slapped a hand on her mouth. "Didn't I

tell you? Mom said she wanted to take me to dinner while she's in town. You know, a mommy-daughter thing. She misses me already."

Marita's heart lurched as panic spread through her. "No, you didn't tell me. You said she was coming here after dinner." She was not going for dinner with Miguel alone. No way, José!

"I thought I did. Sorry."

"Well, you didn't." Marita's voice was sharper than she intended. She knew she was being unfair to Lisa, and in danger of making herself look like a quarrelsome old biddy.

Lisa frowned. "Don't look so angry, Marita. It's no big deal, is it? You go with Miguel and I go with Mom. We both get treated to a meal. Right?"

"I am not angry," Marita said. In fact she was furious. "I'm just—" Totally with no idea how to get out of this predicament.

"We'll be all right, Marita," Miguel said calmly. "I'm sure we can order food without Lisa's guidance."

Feeling foolish for getting flustered, Marita went along with his joke. "I suppose," she said grudgingly. "As long as we don't go to some exotic restaurant where I'll show my ignorance by holding the menu upside down."

"I promise." His voice was soothing. Sensuous. "No exotic restaurants."

"But come to think of it," Marita tried one last, desperate avoidance manoeuvre. "You offered to take us out because the place would be in shambles. But lo! It is totally not in shambles. I can eat at home, no prob."

Lisa opened the fridge door. "Except there's no food in the fridge, besides the left-over pizza," she said pragmatically.

"Oo-kay, then . . ." Marita pursed her lips. No use trying to continue this battle. "How about six thirty?"

"I'll be here," Miguel headed for the door. "Have a nice dinner, Lisa."

After Miguel left, Marita plopped down into the armchair and let the air gush out of her in one long puff. "You could have warned me ahead of time," she said to Lisa.

"Warned you about what?" Lisa sat down on the sofa and swung her legs up, tucking them under her.

"That you were going for dinner with your mother," Marita elucidated patiently. "I wish you'd have told me."

Lisa frowned. "I don't get you, Marita. You almost sound like you don't want to go with Miguel."

Too true. And Marita had no come-back for that.

"He's a totally nice guy," Lisa said comfortingly. "I only met him today, but I like him already."

"And I'm sure he likes you too," Marita forced herself to say. "But you're right. It's no big deal. Let's see if the television works, shall we?"

"And tomorrow I'll find out about the salsa classes," Lisa said, fiddling with the converter. "That'll keep us both from turning into lumpy couch potatoes."

"Oh, yeah, about those salsa classes—"

"It'll be fun, Marita. And like Miguel said, it'll be good for both of us."

"Yeah, I surely do need the exercise."

"We both do."

But Lisa wasn't fooling her. It was plump old Marita who needed the exercise, not willowy young Lisa.

Miguel smiled at Marita, who flipped the pages of

the menu. "This isn't my idea of a casual restaurant," she grumbled. "I wish you'd have warned me, so I would have worn my sequined, strapless evening gown and diamond earrings."

Marita looked so cute with her curls in a casual tumble. He wanted to take her face in his hands and kiss her full mouth that right now was in a pout. He'd brought her to his favourite Spanish restaurant where the tables were covered with white tablecloths and adorned with candles and tasteful arrangements of fresh flowers. He'd reserved this table in a corner, subtly separated from the other diners by a few tall potted plants.

"You think I'd bring my girl to some hamburger joint on our first date?" he said.

Marita's low, earthy laughter bubbled out. He loved the sound and wished he could bring it out more often.

She fingered the white petal of a freesia. "These flowers are real. Not plastic, or even silk, for goodness sake."

"So's the candle," he pointed out. "With a real flame. Classy place, eh?"

"Too classy for me."

Miguel grinned and covered her hand with his. "Well, you're not holding the menu upside down, so it must be all right."

Marita pulled her hand away and began to fiddle with the top button of her white blouse. "But I'm not dressed for this," she said.

"You look beautiful."

She really did. But it wouldn't do to reach over to undo the button she'd just done up, though he sure wanted to. He found the cleavage between her ample breasts enticing, and wanted to see more, not less.

"Did I hear you say I look beautiful?" Marita gave him a sexy glance from under fluttering lashes. "Aw, you're just saying that because it's true."

Miguel looked at her over the rim of his wine glass, "It certainly is. Nothing but the truth."

She was gorgeous, and her figure so appealing that he would have loved to run his hands down her luscious curves. Preferably without a scrap of clothing on her.

To get his mind off such lustful thoughts, he picked up his menu. "Have you looked at the selection?"

"I've looked, but cannot comprehend. That's what you get for bringing me to a Spanish restaurant. So, what's good here?"

"Paella is their specialty," Miguel said. "But I don't know if you'd like that." Jessica would never have chosen paella. "This one has rice and chicken, sausage and shrimp." Too fattening for fussy Jessica. The whole evening would've been taken up with her explaining the reasons she'd chosen such and such a vegetable dish. Dining with Jessica had been a deadly bore. Why he'd suffered living with the woman for three years, he couldn't understand. Not when there were real women like Marita running around free. So sexy and adorable.

"That sounds delicious," Marita said. "I'd love some."

"Great. That's what we'll have then. And, by the way, did I tell you you're adorable?"

The admiration in Miguel's eyes made Marita's breath catch in her throat and she gave an exaggerated cough to cover up her confusion. No mistake about that look, because she could still recognize it even if nothing like it had been directed at her in eons. Maybe at the beginning of her relationship with Ron there might have been a few such looks. And maybe even before that, when she'd gone out with some long-forgotten boyfriend. Yet, even after years of famine, she could tell what a spark of admiration in a man's eyes looked like.

But this evening that look totally took her off guard and she had to pinch her thigh under the table to make sure she wasn't dreaming. It was as real as the flowers on the table and the candle flame, and not just wishful thinking on her part. It confused her. How was she supposed to react to it? Perhaps with a bit of flirtation? Or maybe if she ignored it, it would go away? But across from her sat Miguel, gazing at her with a look that was pretty difficult to ignore, with his white dress shirt casually open at the neck, exposing some smooth, bronzed skin.

Marita decided on flirtation and gulped down some wine to fortify herself. Provocatively she brushed a wisp of hair behind one ear and made an exaggerated moué with her lips. "*Adorable? Moi? Oh, monsieur*!"

Miguel again reached over and took her hand. "*Oui, adorable*. And I like being with you."

So much for her attempt at flirtation. And there went her composure, too.

"I like being with you, too, Miguel," she blurted out before she'd had time to think. But it was the truth. She liked being with him, because she was falling for him. Badly. But what was his excuse?

"I'm so glad to hear that. You had me worried, you know. The way you carried on when Lisa said she was going for dinner with her mother, I was starting to think you didn't want to go with me."

"Alone."

"Pardon?" He frowned, puzzled.

Marita bit her tongue. How did that word slip out? And how to extricate herself from this?

By making it into an exaggerated joke, of course. "I didn't want to be alone with you because I didn't trust you. Since you said I'm so adorable, I figured maybe you wouldn't be able to keep your hands off me."

Miguel laughed. "Well, you got that one right."

She was relieved the waiter appeared to take their order, because she had no idea what she should say to that. She knew he was only responding to her joke with one of his own, but it would have been difficult to think of a smart come-back.

While eating they stayed in safe, comfortable territory, chatting about the food and about her apartment. Thank goodness.

But after they'd finished their meal, complete with Crema Catalana with its burnt sugar topping, Miguel leaned back in his chair, sipped his wine, and dropped the bomb.

"So, about those salsa classes—" he began, but stopped short when he saw Marita's horrified expression.

"Salsa classes?" she exclaimed. "I'm not about to go to any salsa classes, young man."

"But you said—"

"Mere idle conversation. I'm sorry if I misled you." Marita dismissed the subject with a wave of her hand. "I'm not a dancer."

Miguel shook a finger at her. "I beg to differ. You danced the tango beautifully this afternoon."

"Only because years ago I took tango lessons," she persisted. "But as far as salsa is concerned—frankly I do not see how you can possibly dance to a tomato sauce."

Miguel's laughter exploded and reached beyond the palm trees, causing several heads to turn their way.

"Listen," he said. "If you're unsure about going to classes, how about I come and give you a few lessons in the privacy of your home? Then when you feel more comfortable, we can go to the Spadina Salsa Club for an evening of fun, music and dancing."

His deep, dark voice appealed to her. His intense brown eyes appealed to her. His hand, reaching across the table and lightly gripping hers appealed to her. How could she refuse?

She couldn't.

"Well, if Lisa comes along . . ."

Miguel nodded, smiling widely. "Of course. She'll enjoy it too." He looked victorious. "We'll have a couple of lessons to give you a feel for it, and then we'll go to the Salsa Club."

"And you'll be sure to dance with both of us?" Marita willed her voice to not sound needy. She didn't want to end up sitting by herself for the whole evening. No way, José! That would be too much like Ron leaving her to sit while he danced with every lovely lady in the room. Oh well, that was water under the bridge.

No, it wasn't.

"Of course. Though I'm sure Lisa will find many young men who will want to dance with her. Lots of people go to these salsa evenings without partners and look for someone available. And it's even normal to exchange partners."

A few evenings later Miguel came, as promised, to give Marita her first dance lesson. When he walked in, he almost knocked the breath right out of her. With his navy pants and dark blue shirt he looked so handsome, she became totally flustered. But when he took her gently by the shoulders and pulled her into his arms, she almost floated from pure bliss.

With a light kiss on the lips he released her. "Hi Marita," he said.

"Hi, Miguel," she replied hoarsely, took a couple of unsteady steps backwards and quickly turned away. It wouldn't do to gaze at him all dewy-eyed.

"Lisa's in school," Marita told him as she led the way into the living room. "She has an evening class and won't be home till after ten."

Miguel placed a bunch of CDs on the coffee table. "Too bad we won't be able to show her the great progress you'll make tonight."

"Great progress? Sure. If you say so." Marita tried not to sound tremulous. She didn't know if she was ready to have him hold her in his arms. Or whatever one did when dancing salsa. "Okay, so what do we do first?"

Miguel picked up the coffee table and carried it into the kitchen. "First let's turn this room into a dance floor."

They rolled up the area rug and moved the armchair against the wall. He inserted a disc into the CD player and turned off all the lights, except for a table lamp in a corner.

"You ready?" Miguel asked.

Throbbing rhythm filled the room. She'd never felt so self-conscious and vulnerable. To cover up she struck a military pose and saluted smartly. "Ready for action, sir." But she was far from it. With a comical grimace she spread out her palms in a helpless gesture. "Actually I have no idea what I'm supposed to do."

"Don't worry. It'll only hurt if you twist your ankle," he said.

Marita snorted. "Thanks. That's so reassuring."

Miguel began to move his feet and hips to the sultry music and held his arms invitingly toward her.

"Come on," he cajoled. "Just move your body however the music tells you." He continued to move seductively in rhythm, still holding out his hands. "This is Bachata, a slow dance with easy steps."

"I don't even dare to come near you when you move like that." Marita smiled woefully. "You look too sexy."

Miguel grinned. "One, two, three. Five, six, seven," he counted as he stepped back and forth, but Marita still kept her distance.

"What happened to four and eight?" she asked, playing for time.

"For those beats you stand still, kind of. Here let me show you." He stopped the music and came to stand beside her. Taking her left hand in his right one, he proceeded to show her the simple beginner steps.

"One, two, three. Pause. Five, six, seven. Pause. See?"

After only a couple of minutes she was doing it.

"You're a fast learner," Miguel said.

Again he started the music. He held both of her hands, but danced a comfortable distance away from her.

Slowly she relaxed. And soon she found herself smiling, enjoying the way the music made her body move. Her hips gyrated effortlessly to the beat, and she felt like she'd been dancing like this forever.

"You're doing great," he encouraged her.

Marita grinned happily. "The music kind of tells me how to move."

But when Miguel pulled her closer against him, and his right arm went around to her back, she stiffened.

"It's all right," he whispered in her ear and took her right hand into his. "The steps are still the same. Keep on moving to the beat. One, two, three. Pause. Five, six, seven. Pause."

Her breasts pressed against his chest, and he gyrated his hips ever so slightly against her pelvis, making her dizzy.

"Miguel, is this really part of the dance or are you doing something indecent?" She couldn't keep the slight wobble from her voice.

Miguel laughed. "We're perfectly within legal limits. Dancing the Bachata is a real art."

"A real sexy art?"

"Yes."

"O-kay. I think."

But the repetitive steps and pulsing rhythm had the desired effect. Soon Marita felt less self-conscious and allowed her body to respond to Miguel's movements. So when he slid his hand up and down her hip, she was able to respond with sexy undulations.

Her breathing became faster and beads of perspiration formed on her forehead. Whoever said salsa was great exercise was right, because it certainly got her panting. Even though the rhythm was slow, it was sultry. Smouldering hot, in fact. She was almost melting.

Or could it be it was Miguel having this effect on her? With his black hair slicked back, and those dark eyes smiling into hers. With his body-hugging dark shirt that revealed every rippling sinew of his chest and arms. With his pants that left his trim butt and solid thighs for her eyes to consume. Nope. It wasn't only the music.

And once in a while, when those thighs rubbed against hers, slowly, enticingly, it sent the room spinning around her.

"One, two, three, pause. Five six, seven, pause," she counted out loud. But her voice was becoming hoarse.

"You're lovely," Miguel said softly and one arm came up and around her shoulders, pressing her even closer. Marita felt herself drowning. Of course it was only because of the workout from the dance that her breath had gone AWOL. It was not from the words he'd just said in his dark, almost hypnotic voice.

She took a deep breath, grasping at straws. "Speaking of art," she babbled, "I understand Michael and Shaylee are in Paris at the moment, enjoying their honeymoon."

She was afraid he could feel her furiously thumping heart through her thin blouse. "Or maybe they've already left for some other exotic locale." She wanted desperately to press a hand against her breast to calm her heart down. "But what's Mika Laine doing these days?"

Idiotic chatter, when she could have simply enjoyed being in the arms of the man she was crazy about. Why couldn't she just receive this delight handed to her on a silver platter? This whole evening, his arm holding her close, and the feel of every muscle of his hard, sinewy body against hers was all perfectly legal. Or so he'd told her.

But what was happening inside her definitely was not.

Miguel didn't seem to sense anything was amiss. "Mika's working on the photos he took in Africa," he said and whirled her around. "Painting huge canvasses which a business commissioned from him. He's also getting some paintings ready for the Four Winds Gallery, and he'll take over the class this fall if I happen to be busy."

The music ended. Miguel released her and went into the kitchen for a drink of water.

"That's great." Marita's breathing was calming down and when he returned she was ready to face him with a smile. "So, the three Michaels are all doing well?"

"Professionally, yes. But Michael's the only one whose love life is in order. Mika's a carefree bachelor, and I don't think there's anything in his plans to change that." With no trace of joking in his voice he looked Marita in the eye. "Personally, I'm looking for a more meaningful relationship."

"Are you, now?" Marita had to look down to inspect a loose thread on the button hole of her blouse. "And you haven't found anyone yet?" Did that come out casually enough? She hoped so.

"I think I may have," Miguel replied.

"That's really great." It was totally not great. If she wasn't careful, the bright, approving grin she'd painted on her face would wobble and turn upside down. "I assume it's not anyone I know?" Like Lisa, maybe?

"Don't assume." He still looked at her, but his face remained serious.

Marita raised her hands, palms out. "Sorry. It was mere idle curiosity. No need to be offended." God, why was he taking her light, innocent question so seriously? Obviously he didn't want to go there. But it had to be Lisa, of course. He said he may have found someone, and it was someone she knew, so—

"I'm not offended. Shall we continue?" Miguel slipped another disk into the CD player. He held out his hand to her, and she took it with trepidation.

Yes, she wanted his arms around her. Yes, she wanted him to hold her close against him. But darn it all, if he had some woman, maybe Lisa, picked out for a meaningful relationship . . .

Suddenly the glow was gone from the evening. This was all so ridiculous. He was only doing what he'd said he would, teach her a few steps before taking her and Lisa to the Spadina Salsa Club for some fun exercise. And here she was, practically having an orgasm in his arms.

Lady, get a grip!

They continued to dance but now Marita held her emotions tightly in check. Naturally that affected her movements which were no longer as free and easy.

Miguel looked concerned. "You look tired, Marita," he said after they'd danced a few more minutes. "Maybe we should call it a night. I don't want you to be totally bushed at work tomorrow."

Marita wiped her forehead. "You're right. Time to roll back the rug."

Miguel pushed the armchair into place. "We should probably try to have another lesson before we go to the salsa club on Friday, but there's only tomorrow night."

"I'm okay with that," Marita replied. "I can catch up on my work on the weekend."

Miguel went into the hall and picked up his jacket. "Got a big project on the go?"

"I need to get the menus ready for a couple of functions next month. No big deal." Yes, Miguel was still the big deal and trumped all but the most necessary things in her life at this moment.

That, despite what he'd just told her about having an eye on someone for a meaningful relationship. Was she a fool for punishment or what?

Miguel zipped up his jacket and then took her in his arms. "See you tomorrow night," he said and planted a quick kiss on her lips.

Chapter Four

"Triple M Graphic Design and Production" was located downtown on the main floor of one of the many century homes, which had been converted into office spaces. The room was silent, as Miguel and Mika sat at their respective tables, each absorbed in his project.

Miguel raised his head and put down his pencil. "You know, Mika, I think I'm in love," he announced. He had to tell someone.

Mika turned to look at his friend. "No kidding? Have you and Jessica got back together again?

Jessica? Now why would Mika ask that? "No, it's not Jessica," Miguel replied impatiently. "She moved out last summer. Or don't you remember?"

"I remember," Mika said. "But since you haven't mentioned any other women in your life, I thought maybe you'd got together again. After all, you were together for . . . how long? Three years?"

"That was two years too long," Miguel said, yawning. "The only thing we had in common was salsa."

"No sex?"

"Sex? Of course, sex," Miguel again replied impatiently, dropping his pencil on the floor. He bent down to pick it up. "But that was never anything to write home about."

"Oh? And now you've found someone you can write home about?"

"Yes, I think I have."

Mika slipped off his stool and walked to the kitchenette to pour himself a cup of coffee from a thermos carafe. "Am I going to find out her name, or are you going to keep all the details a secret?"

"Her name is Marita Osborne."

Mika frowned thoughtfully as he sipped his coffee. "Marita Osborne? Haven't I heard that name before?"

"Probably. She's Shaylee's girlfriend," Miguel told him. "And although you weren't at the wedding, maybe you heard Michael or Shaylee mention her at some point. She was in the art class last spring, and that's where I met her. I took over the class for a couple of weeks when Michael had to go to Montréal to oversee the work on the mural he'd designed."

Mika nodded. "Okay, that's probably it. Funny you haven't mentioned her before since you've known her this long."

"I didn't see her after the classes ended in June. Frankly, I didn't know much about her, except she was Shaylee's friend. She could've been married, for all I knew, and the mother of a brood of kids. But somehow I couldn't stop thinking about her all summer."

Dreaming about her was more like it. Wishing he could hear her low, earthy laughter again and chuckle at her humorous expressions. And see the enticing cleavage of her breasts as she bent over the art table, absorbed in her work. Her work? Miguel had to smile. It was hardly a step above what a grade-school kid would have painted, and she'd certainly been aware of that. But she'd still been keen to try.

But back to her cleavage. There was something different about her cleavage, as compared to the deliberate show of breast of the other women in the class. Marita was soft and natural, totally unaware of her charms and how they affected him.

Mika laughed. "And now that you know she's neither married nor a mother, you want to make her both of the above?"

Miguel didn't join in the laughter. "Well, I don't know how she feels about being a mother, but I'm certainly going to see if she's willing to date me. And marry me, eventually."

Mika sobered up. "This does sound serious." He slipped up to sit on his stool.

"Yes." Miguel gave a few sharp taps on the table with his pencil. "I love this woman," he said firmly. "And I'm going to have her."

Mika chuckled. "It sounds a bit odd to me, you chasing after a woman. As long as I've known you, you've always been the chasee, not the chaser, where women are concerned."

Miguel laughed. "I guess that's probably true. But I'm afraid to rush her, because I sense she's kind of unsure of herself. I know her husband left her and it looks to me like she's lost her self-confidence. I feel she's vulnerable. Wounded. If you know what I mean. She doesn't know how attractive she is and tries so hard to make like she doesn't care. She keeps joking, but I can sense it's only a cover-up for her insecurities."

Mika bowed his head to Miguel. "Dr. Freud, I presume?"

Miguel shot his friend a frown. "Okay, so don't take

me seriously," he said. "But I mean it. I want her."

"I guess that means you're not taking advantage of the hospitality of the ladies in the art class, like Michael was doing before Shaylee enchanted him?"

"That's right. I'm not."

"Not even for some occasional amusement?"

"Not interested. Jessica was enough to put me off women like that forever."

Mika laughed. "Me, I'm looking forward to taking over the classes next fall, so I can take advantage of the perks that go along with it. Unless I get accepted at the Helsinki University as a guest lecturer for the fall semester." He aimed an eraser and threw it at Miguel. "Now quit mooning over this fabulous woman of yours and let me get back to work."

"Hey, you're the one who's asking the questions," Miguel retorted. He bent over his drafting table, but it was Marita's laughing face that looked up at him instead of the ad he was supposed to be designing.

"One, two, three. Five six, seven," Miguel counted.

Marita caught the beat quickly and began to sway as her feet moved in time with the music.

She noticed Miguel held her even closer tonight than the previous time, and as the music beat out its entrancing rhythm, his moves became more daring. He held her against him and one hand slid down her back, to caress her buttocks.

"Is this still legal?" Marita breathed. It felt wonderful, and she hoped he would say yes.

He did. "It's all legal," he murmured and his lips brushed lightly against her cheek. "Tomorrow night at the club you'll see everybody doing it."

He had her pirouette slowly around in front of him

a few times, but Marita didn't need this to make her any more dizzy than she already was simply from being near him. Again he pulled her close and this time he brought his mouth down to nuzzle her neck. The caress was soft as a butterfly's kiss, but it was as though his lips had ravaged her, the way they made her pulse quicken and the blood pound inside her.

Every few minutes, as his moves became more and more tantalizing, she had to keep reminding herself what Miguel had said. Everyone did this. This didn't mean anything. He wasn't making love to her. He was simply dancing salsa. But what the heck, she could enjoy the ride, no matter what his motivation was for doing all these lovely things to her.

When the dance was over, Miguel changed the CD for a faster piece. Marita was able to keep up quite well—at least she thought so—and found that with the faster rhythms they danced farther apart, preventing him from doing all those seductively sexy moves on her.

But then he put on a slow Bachata recording. Swaying his hips, he took both her hands in his and pulled her close. Very close. And then he slipped his knee between her thighs. Marita froze. Her feet stopped obeying her and she stumbled.

"Sorry, I—" In her panic she took a step back and her foot hit the edge of the rolled up rug, sending her flying backwards. Her head bumped against the cushion on the edge of the couch and she slid gently onto the floor.

Miguel hadn't let go of her and followed her down. He was able to grab the edge of the couch with one hand to break his fall so his landing on top of her was soft. And delicious. Marita had a wild desire to spread open her legs and have him there, right where she wanted him. Preferably naked, of course.

"Are you okay," Miguel asked, but didn't move. He braced himself up on both elbows.

"I'm fine," Marita replied. "Did I just invent a new salsa move, or is this also something couples do all the time?"

Miguel grinned, flashing his white teeth. "We don't usually dance salsa lying down. But this is a tried and true position for other purposes."

He was going to kiss her. Marita knew from the glint in his dark eyes. And she was going to let him. She couldn't help it. Slowly she closed her eyes and brought her chin up a fraction of an inch. For a second his mouth hovered above hers, and then their lips touched. Soft and delicious at first, the kiss soon deepened when she opened her mouth to him. It was exactly the way she'd imagined his kiss to be whenever she allowed herself to indulge in silly, futile daydreams. He kissed her so thoroughly, so intensely, Marita thought she would sink right through the floor boards and land in the living room of the surprised tenants in the apartment below. She couldn't remember ever having been kissed like that. Maybe because she never had. The experience was unreal. Total ecstasy.

Miguel drew back with a deep sigh. "The next step, if I remember correctly from my sex manual, would be for me to start undressing you. But maybe we're a bit too early in our relationship for that much intimacy?"

Marita wasn't sure she could talk yet, but made an attempt at a joke. Her voice came out in a croak. "You kidding? Obviously you didn't catch on that I stumbled on purpose to get you on top of me for that exact purpose. Subtle move, eh?"

Oh, how she wanted to keep him right there. For the whole night, if possible.

Miguel laughed. "No, I didn't catch on. But I'm flattered."

To her regret he got up and extended his hand to help her up on her feet.

"Thanks," Marita said with a deliberately audible grunt. "Us older ladies need a bit of assistance in these situations."

"I was being chivalrous," Miguel said. "Nothing to do with age. But next time I'll let you scramble up on your own."

Next time? If only.

"Maybe we should call it a night," Marita suggested, stretching as though she was totally exhausted. She wasn't. "At my age, I don't want to overdo it." God, why did she always have to go there? Was she an incurable idiot or what?

"Salsa dancing takes more out of you than you realize," Miguel said, and added, "At any age."

The door opened and Lisa marched in.

"Hi Miguel, Marita," she caroled. "How's the dance lesson going? Sorry I missed it." She dropped her backpack heavily on the hall floor.

"Your aunt is a natural," Miguel said and put an arm around Marita's shoulders. "If it weren't so late we'd show you."

The arm weighed a ton. Like a ton of sweet honey. Marita slipped out from under it. "Next time we'll give you an exhibition," she said.

"You two look a bit shaken up," Lisa observed. "Too much action?"

"Yes, you could say that," Marita muttered while

Miguel, hiding a grin, went to stop the music.

"How do you get exercise by dancing to that?" Lisa asked. "It sounded so slow. Sultry even."

Marita coughed to hide a giggle. "You'd be surprised."

Ron called again. For the second time this week. What the hell was the matter with the man?

"Ron," Marita said firmly into the phone. "I do not want you coming around here any more. I don't want to be rude, but we've been divorced for three years. And in case you don't remember, it was over between us way before that."

"But is there any reason why we can't still be friends?" Ron sounded wounded. "I mean, just because we're divorced, can't a guy drop by once in a while to chat? Or something?"

Good Lord, was the man actually whining?

A few months ago she had kindly, but obviously mistakenly, offered him dinner when he'd "happened" to drop by at six o'clock. Unfortunately that was like feeding a stray cat, because now his dinner-time visits were occurring with greater and greater frequency.

"No. I don't want you to come here any more."

"What?" Now he sounded shocked. "We were married for seventeen years and we shared so much— shared everything. And now you want us to behave like strangers?"

Marita had to laugh at his nerve. "Ron, you really are incredible."

He obviously took her laughter as a sign of consent. "I'll be right there," he said quickly and hung up before she had a chance to object.

Damn the man! How rude did she have to be so he

would get the message? She'd never asked what was going on in his marriage to cause these forays into her life, because she didn't want to give him the idea she was the least bit interested in his affairs.

Quickly she dialed his number, but he didn't pick up. He had probably been calling from the downstairs lobby, because the next moment there he was, knocking. Marita sighed and opened the door for him. Miguel was coming to pick up her and Lisa for the salsa club, and they were planning to grab a quick bite at a restaurant before the dance.

"Who let you in?" she asked as rudely as possible, but couldn't help smiling at his disappointed face when he saw the empty stovetop.

"No dinner tonight?" was his first comment.

Could it have been more obvious as to why he'd come?

"Lisa and I are eating out. You might as well turn right around and go home."

But instead Ron strode into the living room and plopped into the armchair. "I could join you."

"No." Marita said bluntly. "That wouldn't be convenient. So, please don't make yourself comfortable."

Lisa came out of her room. "Hi, Uncle Ron," she said and threw a questioning look toward Marita.

At that point the phone rang and Lisa went to buzz Miguel up. A few moments later he entered. As usual, a rush of pleasure coursed through Marita at the sight of him.

"Hi Miguel," she said sweetly. Now would have been the perfect time for him to take her in his arms and kiss her hello.

But he didn't. Unfortunately.

"Miguel, this is Ron, my—" she began, but just then Ron broke in.

"Miguel? How are you, young man," he boomed, getting up. "I'm glad to see Lisa has already got herself a nice boyfriend. Trust my niece. Heh, heh."

Lisa looked flustered. "Uncle Ron, Miguel isn't my boyfriend."

Ron's laugh was a loud, suggestive cackle that made Marita cringe. "He isn't? Well, you should pick up your socks, young man. This lovely young lady isn't going to last very long in Toronto."

Marita grimaced. He had to keep using the word "young". Damn him! Had she always been so overly conscious of that adjective, or just since Miguel had come into her life? Probably not, but these days the word seemed to pop up all the time. It made her feel extremely self-conscious and uncomfortable. And old.

Miguel came over to Marita and put an arm around her shoulders. "I'm here to pick up these two lovely ladies for dinner," he said. His grip tightened imperceptibly and Marita had to fight the urge to look smug.

Ron was obviously taken aback by this gesture. "Oh? Well, I guess I should be getting along," he blustered. "If Martha doesn't have time to chat with me tonight."

"If you hadn't hung up on me so fast I could have told you not to bother coming up," Marita said and went to open the door for him.

With slumped shoulders Ron headed for the elevator. God, how dejected could he make himself look. "Maybe another time." Marita couldn't stop herself from calling after him.

A few minutes later, in Miguel's car, he asked, "Does

your husband come over often?"

"My ex-husband," Marita corrected him. "For some reason he's been coming over a lot more lately, usually arriving conveniently in time for dinner."

Lisa giggled. "I think Uncle Ron isn't too happy with his wife's cooking."

"The only thing Ron never complained about was my cooking." This was the first time Marita had divulged anything to Miguel about her marriage.

"I can't see what's to complain about you. I think you're perfect," Miguel stated firmly.

"Yeah, I know. I'm like Mary Poppins, practically perfect in every way." Marita was gratified when Lisa and Miguel both laughed. It was always safe to hide behind a joke.

"I mean it," Miguel said. "You're the greatest."

"Oh, pshaw!" Marita lowered her face dramatically. "There you go again, saying things only because they're true." The heat rising to her face was genuine.

When Miguel had parked the car and they neared the doors of the Spadina Salsa Club, Marita heard the familiar Latin music pour out the open doors. She swallowed hard and willed her stomach to keep down the spaghetti and shrimp she'd consumed for dinner. Was she ready to put herself on show to the whole world? Or at least to a roomful of experienced salsa dancers?

But, hey, Ron wouldn't be there. She wouldn't have to put up with the degradation of having him enviously ogle the slender, young dancers in the arms of other, luckier-than-he, guys. Even when dancing with her, Ron had never looked at Marita, except to scowl at her when their toes bumped. And it had always been her fault. No debating it.

"This is so exciting," Lisa squealed. "Doesn't the music make you want to move?"

"Yeah, makes me want to turn around and move right out of here," Marita muttered.

After paying the entrance fee, Miguel led them into the dimly lit dance hall where beams of coloured lights flitted among the undulating bodies. He found them a round table by the wall and went to get drinks from the bar.

Marita gulped with growing trepidation. The dancers, their beautiful bodies glistening with perspiration, gyrated and swayed, sometimes glued against each other, sometimes moving tantalizingly apart. In the privacy of her living room she'd been able to become more free with her movements. And yesterday, during the second lesson, she'd even raised her arms high, instead of having them flop around by her sides. Right from the start her hips had somehow naturally followed the music without much effort on her part, and Miguel's raised eyebrows had boosted her self-confidence. His appreciative "Wow!" still echoed sweetly in her ears. But was she ready for this?

After watching the dancing for a few minutes Miguel rose and extended his hand to Marita. "Ready?" he said with an encouraging smile.

Did he sense how nervous she was? Sense? Nervousness was probably oozing out of her pores, if that was physically possible.

"Why don't you dance with Lisa first," Marita suggested. "I want to watch for a while, if you don't mind. You know, suck in the ambiance."

"Sure." Miguel nodded and led Lisa to the dance floor. Marita watched them with growing envy. They were such a great fit. Lisa had been learning the basic steps on her own from a salsa video with a bit of guidance from Marita, and now she seemed to dance like a pro. Of course it was mainly because Miguel was such a fabulous leader, so it was easy to follow him.

It looked like they were dancing so close that Lisa probably could feel the pressure of Miguel's thigh rubbing against her crotch. Marita well knew that sensation, and remembered how the heat had thrust into her with a force that left her almost panting. And his hips gyrating against her pelvis—now against Lisa's—had sent her soaring to the moon and beyond.

It would have been easy to imagine he was doing these moves with Lisa because he cared about the girl and felt sexy with her, but of course it was only the dance. Marita knew that. But watching Miguel execute the same moves with Lisa as he'd done with her, seeing him press his lips against Lisa's cheek and—she could only imagine—tasting her, that was a most uncomfortable feeling. The fact that other dancers were doing same kinds of moves made her feel only marginally better.

When Miguel and Lisa returned to the table, they were laughing at some joke.

"Honestly I'm glad we brought along those extra tops," Lisa said to Marita as she sat down. "I'm already hot and we only danced a couple of sets."

Marita laughed. "I'm ready to change mine, too. I got hot just watching all these people moving their hips in such a wild way. It looked like they were having sex standing up. Whew! I could swear they're all lovers. You guys included."

Miguel placed a hand on her shoulder. "It's the way salsa's danced. I'll bet some of those people aren't even dancing with the person they came with tonight. There could be a husband dancing with someone else's wife, and vice versa."

"Seems to me that's solid grounds for divorce," Marita muttered.

"Yeah, a person walking in here, who didn't know about salsa, would think there's something indecent going on," Lisa mused.

The music started again. This time, without asking for her consent, Miguel took Marita's hand. "Our dance," he announced and pulled her up and onto the dance floor.

He immediately captured both her hands in his and brought them up above her head, making her feel captured and vulnerable. Marita could do nothing but helplessly stare as Miguel's hips in his tight black jeans started to move slowly back and forth in rhythm with the music.

God! He was imitating the sex act. Heat rushed down into the pit of her stomach. She couldn't look away.

"One, two, three. Five, six, seven," Miguel chanted softly, mesmerizing her. "One, two, three. Five, six, seven."

Did he expect her to concentrate on counting while he was provocatively thrusting himself at her like that?

He turned her hands making her twirl around in front of him. And around. And around. When he stopped her to face him again, she was dizzy. And it wasn't only from the turns.

Tentatively she began to move her hips to the beat. Why fight it? Might as well try to enjoy this. When he freed her hands, she raised them above her head and crossed them at the wrists, splaying her fingers, like she'd seen many of the women do. Undulating her hips, she hesitantly stepped closer to Miguel and saw an approving glint in his eyes.

"Way to go, girl," he murmured, and twirled around, stopping with his legs apart in front of her, knees bent.

"Come here, you." He turned her so her back was toward him.

Marita stopped breathing as, with his hands splayed across her stomach, he pulled her bottom against his pelvis and pressed her closer.

"One, two, three," she counted aloud when she was able to breathe again. "Right? Five, six, seven."

"Right," Miguel murmured in her ear. "You've got it."

"C-could have fooled me," Marita stuttered as he ground himself against her. "I don't think I'm dancing any more."

"What are you doing?" he asked softly, seduction dripping in his voice.

Having virtual sex with him, that's what!

They continued to dance, to twirl and gyrate, until Marita knew if this went on for a second longer she would have an orgasm. Or she would melt. Not from exertion, but from the heat of the sexy moves.

"Time out," she gasped, turning back to face Miguel. She walked unsteadily toward their table and flopped down onto her chair, totally out of breath. "Whew! That sure takes a toll on you. You go ahead and continue with someone else, Miguel. I see Lisa's hooked herself a man already."

Miguel stood by her chair, hesitating. "If you're sure—?"

"I'm positive," she assured him. "It's only my first night out, so—" Liar! She did not want him to dance with anyone else. Lisa, maybe, but not with any of the other willowy, curvaceous women.

"Miguel, I thought it was you!" A gorgeous young woman appeared from nowhere and slipped her arms around Miguel's waist. She wore a skin-tight miniskirt that flared out at the hem, and her halter-top was cut so low it barely covered her nipples.

She gave him a resounding kiss on the mouth.

Miguel's laugh sounded a bit forced as he wiped his mouth. "Jessica, fancy seeing you here."

Marita wanted to think he'd wiped away the kiss, but it could be he just wanted to remove the lipstick.

"Yes, fancy that, all right," the woman said with a bright laugh. "Where else would I be on a Friday night? You know I practically live here, darling. Just like we used to."

Marita watched the exchange with growing dismay. Who was this Jessica? This drop-dead beauty.

"Marita, I'd like you to meet Jessica. We're . . . old friends." The little catch in his voice didn't escape Marita. "Jess, this is Marita."

Old friends, eh?

"Delighted to meet you," Jessica cooed, but her eyes said she was far from delighted. "Actually, I'm Miguel's ex."

Oh? And had they split up because she left him, or vice versa?

Jessica took Miguel by the hand and started to pull him to the dance floor. "Come on. Let's see if we still have it."

Of course Miguel went along. Hadn't Marita told him to go dance with someone else? But, hey, that did not include his ex.

Much as she wanted to, Marita couldn't take her eyes off them. Dammit! Yes, they still had it. Marita could have kicked herself. If she hadn't been so totally overwhelmed by Miguel's dance moves, she could now be dancing with him instead of watching him twirl enticingly with that young and slim thing. God, the woman didn't even need a bra.

How good they looked together. Miguel was right into the dance, thrusting his hips, sliding his hands down her body and Marita couldn't turn her head away even though her vision was becoming blurred. She brushed a hand across her eyes, but continued to stare, mesmerized. Miguel seemed to be enjoying himself. Way too much.

"Excuse me," a deep male voice beside her forced Marita to stop torturing herself and look around. A middle-aged man bowed politely to her. He was slightly on the heavy side, with graying temples.

"I couldn't help but notice how well you danced a few moments ago. Would you allow me to lead you in this dance?"

Chapter Five

Marita hesitated for only a second. Hell, why not? There was Miguel having a great time with—of all people—his ex-girlfriend.

"I'd love to," she said brightly and rose, giving the man her hand.

He led her to the dance floor and Marita fully expected him to take her in the traditional dance pose. Instead he took her hands in his and swung her around.

"Let's boogie," he said and began to swing his hips to the music.

It was plain to see he wasn't a novice, and Marita found it very easy to follow him. One, two, three. Pause. Five, six, seven. Pause. After a while she even stopped counting and miraculously was still able to keep to the rhythm.

And what's more, she was enjoying herself, letting down her guard like she hadn't been able to do with Miguel. The dance continued, the music throbbed a sexy beat, and she was full of joyful vigour as she undulated her hips enticingly. She rubbed herself against the thigh he thrust between her legs, and when he turned her around, she ground her butt against his groin. She no longer cared if she didn't follow the exact sequence of steps. Counting be damned. Eight, three, ten. Pause. Four, six, nine and a half. This was fun!

At last she asked the gentleman to take her back to her table. This time her exhaustion was for real and she dabbed the perspiration off her forehead with a tissue, trying not to collapse into her chair too awkwardly.

"Thank you," she gasped with a big smile. "That was great."

"My name is Steve Applebaum," the man said. "I hope I may dance with you again tonight."

"Marita Osborne," she said.

Steve sat down in Miguel's chair. "May I?"

"You just did."

Steve laughed. "In order to make sure I don't lose track of you, if we don't get to dance again, would it be possible for me to jot down your phone number?"

"Well . . ." Marita demurred. "I don't think you and I are ready for such intimacies yet. Maybe another time?"

Miguel returned to the table, looking serious. Maybe even vexed? He nodded briefly as Steve got up and surrendered the chair.

Had something happened between Miguel and Jessica to produce the scowl on Miguel's face? Maybe they had quarreled?

But, frankly, she didn't want to know about the ups and downs of their relationship. It was no skin off her nose.

"Steve, this is Miguel." Come to think of it, exactly what was Miguel to her? If she told Steve he was her former art teacher it would give a totally wrong impression of her artistic talents.

"My dance instructor," she added after a pause, because that's what Miguel was. All they'd ever done was practised dancing.

"Really?" Steve turned to Miguel. "You've done a fabulous job, my friend. She's great."

"Thanks," Miguel said shortly. His annoyed expression didn't change.

"Miguel has been teaching me to dance salsa so I can get some exercise."

"Exercise is good for us all," Steve said, and then added some very unfortunate words. "Especially as we near middle age."

Marita's heart took a skydive. Right on, Steve-baby. But she soldiered on and didn't bat an eyelash as she said, "You're right on the button there, Steve."

But Steve was quick to pull the buns out of the fire. "I'm talking about myself, of course. Neither of you is even close to middle age. Me, I have adult children, for heaven's sake."

Marita swallowed. Her child would be going to kindergarten this fall. If only she hadn't rushed down the steps in those spiky heels. That horrible fall. She looked down at her hands to hide her eyes from the men. The miscarriage was her own fault and she would never forgive herself for it. But what had killed it for her was Ron's reaction.

"Whew, that was a close one," he'd exclaimed when he came to see her in the hospital. And he had promptly gone to get a vasectomy. Which was fine, because after that comment she never wanted to have a baby with him. He would have made a real loving daddy, all right!

Marita shook herself free of the unhappy memories as Miguel took her hand, a signal to Steve they intended to dance.

"I do hope I'll see you here again next week, Marita. And you're doing a great job teaching her, Miguel," Steve repeated.

"Right."

Miguel's terse reply surprised Marita. He should've been pleased at the compliment.

"I believe we'll be here," she said to Steve, and turned to Miguel. "Right?"

"If you wish," Miguel said.

Dammit! Just because he and Jessica had quarrelled, he didn't have to make himself unpleasant to everyone else around him.

When Steve left, Miguel led Marita to the dance floor.

"It was a lot of fun dancing with Steve," she told him cheerfully.

"Good."

They danced, but trying to swivel temptingly in front of a grouch was no fun. After a few minutes she stopped. "Actually, I'm really bushed," she said. She wasn't.

"You want to go home?"

No, she didn't want to go home yet. But she didn't feel like dancing with a grumpy partner who had obviously had an argument with his ex.

"Lisa's still having a good time, so we shouldn't leave yet," she said. "But would it be possible to dance slowly? Maybe skip every other beat or something?"

Miguel put his arm around her waist and pulled her close. "We could do that," he said and took some long, slow steps, holding her in the traditional dance position. She placed her left hand on his shoulder and was dying to let her fingers play with the hair at the nape of his neck. But since he was stewing about Jessica, he probably wouldn't find the move very appealing.

"This is nice," Marita murmured against his chest. "Old-fashioned dancing."

Of course she had to throw that in. One must never let an occasion go by without bringing the word "old" into the conversation. Or one's weight, for that matter. Must one? Damn! It would've been too difficult to kick herself without possibly wounding Miguel, so instead she took herself virtually by the scruff of the neck gave herself a good shake. Idiot!

Miguel laid his cheek against hers and then her world suddenly did a wild handspring. He was sucking at her earlobe, earring and all.

"Marita," he murmured into her ear. "I didn't like watching you dance with that Steve guy."

With him nibbling at her ear, Marita wasn't sure she'd heard him right. "You—you didn't?" she stammered.

"No, I didn't. You looked like you were too much into him." His mouth moved lower and his lips brushed her neck.

Wow! Marita was thankful Miguel's hand was planted solidly on her back, because she was afraid she would collapse into a big fat heap right there on the dance floor.

What exactly was he saying to her? Well, whatever it was, it made her feel too wonderful to start analyzing it right at this moment. Later, in bed, she probably wouldn't be able to stop herself from going over his words with a fine-tooth comb. For now she simply wanted to enjoy the moment, and let the devil take tomorrow.

"But that's the way everyone dances," she murmured. "You told me yourself it's the way salsa is danced. It looks like the people are in love or something, but it's only the dance moves. Right?"

"I know, but I still didn't like to see this fellow all over you. It made me jealous."

"But that's how you were dancing with Jessica," she pointed out.

"And were you jealous?" he asked, his brown eyes teasing her.

"Jealous? Moi? Hah!" Damned right she'd been jealous.

She wished she could have shut off the persistent little voices telling her she was dancing with a man ten years her junior. Or that he weighed less that she did. Or that he and his ex had danced like they were still in love. Because right now he was dancing with her. And he was brushing his beautiful lips against her neck. And he was holding her so tightly she could feel the length of his exquisitely lithe, hard body against her.

It was wonderful to have a man say sweet nothings to her again, even if they were only brought on by the dancing. And she was determined to enjoy that long-forgotten feeling of being wanted.

They were almost standing still among all the feverishly twisting hot bodies. Miguel's gaze lingered on her lips and she knew he was going to kiss her. Slowly he brought his mouth down, sweet and soft against hers. His tongue sought entrance into her, and willingly Marita opened her mouth to him. Slowly Miguel deepened the kiss, until the pounding in her ears turned to a deafening roar and Marita was certain she would swoon like the maidens of old, right here on the dance floor.

The probing, searching kiss was the sexiest, the most delicious thing she'd ever experienced in her life. And when he finally raised his head Marita could tell from the black desire burning in his eyes, and from the way his body was reacting, that he'd also been affected by it. His eyes asked her a question. The question.

Would she have sex with him?

This brought Marita to her senses. This fun could only be allowed to go so far. Dancing was one thing. The odd kiss was another. But sex was something else altogether. After all, only a week ago he'd told her he had someone in mind for a meaningful relationship. Obviously he was only testing her, seeing if an overweight woman who was tottering toward middle age would want to have hot sex with him.

Sure, maybe he was the kind of man who, just for fun, might have casual sex with her. But she knew damned well that nothing lasting was in the cards even if he hadn't had someone meaningful in mind. The minute another young, beautiful body caught his eye, Marita would find herself back at home watching late-night re-runs.

With Miguel she could never consent to being some trivial amusement for him because—she didn't even try to kid herself—she loved him. But if she was desperate for sex, maybe her new friend, Steve, could be enticed to provide her with a casual affair.

Slowly they walked back to the table where Lisa was already sitting.

"Hey, you two," she called over the noise of the

music. "I saw that hot kiss. Now fess up, are you two a number?"

"Lisa!" Marita cried. "That's an inappropriate thing to ask. Haven't you noticed how everyone kisses on the dance floor?" Because that's all the kiss had been. Marita sat down trying to look annoyed, but the glow inside her made it difficult to play angry.

Lisa looked abashed. "I'm sorry, Marita. But you guys weren't actually dancing salsa, so the kiss seemed different, somehow."

"Well, it wasn't." Marita snapped. "It was only part of the dance."

Miguel had been standing silently by the table during this exchange, neither agreeing with nor refuting Marita's explanation. But now he spoke up, and his words almost made Marita fall off her chair.

"Well, I don't know about your aunt," he said slowly, addressing Lisa. He pulled out his chair and turned it so his elbows rested on the back. "But I did it because I wanted to kiss her. It had nothing to do with the dance."

"Miguel!" Marita blustered. Did her blush show in the dim lighting? "Please stop trying to be funny. That's my department."

"I wasn't being funny," he said. "I wanted to kiss you. And I think you wanted me to kiss you."

Lisa followed this exchange, her eyes sparkling with interest. "I knew it," she exclaimed jubilantly. "I could see it."

Marita jumped up from her chair, almost upsetting it in the process. "Okay, you two, I've heard enough nonsense this evening. I don't find this funny. Time to depart."

She had no trouble looking angry now. She couldn't

simply sit there while Miguel made those dumb statements. Someone "meaningful" was already waiting on the back burner, so obviously he wasn't serious when he whispered sweet nothings in her ear and asked if she was jealous. She didn't want to believe he was the kind of man who would play with a woman's emotions, so this all had to be his idea of a joke. If he had known how she felt about him, the joke would have been cruel and callous. But he didn't know.

She could hear Lisa and Miguel following her as she marched with determined steps out of the building and to the parking lot. Surely Miguel hadn't meant to be unkind. Surely he assumed Marita wouldn't take his words seriously. He had just been playing. He was, after all, a handsome, slightly selfish young man who probably was used to teasing women and even accustomed to having his way with them.

In the car she sat like a storm cloud, refusing to speak to either of the two, despite their attempts to get her to relent.

Miguel placed his hand on her knee. "I'm sorry, Marita. I honestly didn't mean to upset you."

She didn't respond.

Lisa reached from the back seat and placed a placating hand on Marita's shoulder. "I'm sorry I said those silly things about the kiss. Please don't be angry with me. I was only teasing."

It was too difficult to continue sulking, with both of them begging for her forgiveness. She patted Lisa's hand. "I forgive you both. But I can't imagine why you made such a fuss over a simple kiss."

Let her make the fuss. Let her relish every second of it and let her relive it a hundred times tonight in the loneliness of her bed.

Marita had just had a leisurely bath and had wrapped herself in a big fluffy towel when the phone rang. She rushed to pick it up, hoping it was Miguel calling. Not that she expected him to call, but maybe—for no reason at all—he would.

It was Steve.

"How on earth did you get my phone number?" Marita asked, after he had identified himself. Droplets of water fell to the floor at her feet.

There was a smile in Steve's voice. "You've heard of the internet? Great place to find people's phone numbers. And there aren't that many Marita Osbornes in Toronto, you know."

"Never thought of that."

"I hope you don't mind. I've been thinking about you since Friday and finally decided to bite the bullet and look you up."

"And so you found me. It all sounds very intriguing." Now, why on earth did she have to say such leading words and maybe put funny ideas into the man's head? Maybe because she was standing there, totally naked except for the towel.

"Yes, I think so, too. And now that I've found you, I wanted to ask if you'd come to a salsa evening with me this Wednesday. There's a salsa club I sometimes go to on Davenport."

A date? She was being asked for a date? The first one in . . . how many years?

"I'm sorry. I can't," she said. Miguel was coming for their usual salsa class. It could, of course, be changed to another night, but—

"That's too bad." The regret in Steve's voice sounded very real. "How about Friday at the Spadina?"

"Can't. Sorry."

"Are you trying to give me the brush off, by any chance?"

"No, honestly, I'm not. It's just that Miguel and I are going on Friday to the Spadina." Marita tried to give her hair a rub with one hand while holding the phone with the other. The towel dropped to the floor and her nudity made her feel vulnerable. "And since you and I have only met once, and very briefly at that, I think it would be rather foolhardy of me to go out with you." After all, she didn't know this Steve from Jack-the-Infamous-Ripper.

"You're right, of course. It was pretty stupid of me to call like this. You'd think at my age I would have thought about that." He gave a short laugh. "But I guess I consider myself such a non-threatening guy that I don't think in those terms." He was silent for a moment. "How about we meet for dinner at some restaurant? Some place convenient for you. Would that be all right? Say, on Thursday night?"

He wasn't exactly pleading, but he sounded like he really, really wanted to go out with her. Could she say no to such an ardent fellow? It sounded innocent enough. Dinner in a restaurant of her choosing. Surrounded by waitresses who knew her.

"Sure, that sounds good, Steve."

After telling him the name of the restaurant she hung up, feeling a bit giddy at the thought of going for dinner with a virtual stranger. Especially as she was standing in the middle of the room wet and stark naked.

What would Miguel think about this? Or, more realistically, why would Miguel think anything about this? After all, she and Miguel were only acquaintances. Kind of. Just because he kissed her whenever they met, it didn't mean anything. Her old uncle Fred always kissed her when they met. Her brother-in-law, Harry, always kissed her when they met. She could name any number of men who kissed her when they met. She was the foolish one to whom Miguel's kisses meant anything. To him they were simply a custom. And the kisses at the salsa club were part of the dance, no matter what silly nonsense he'd spouted when they were dancing.

Marita picked up her towel and slowly began to dry herself.

But the kiss sure had felt wonderful. If only Miguel were now rubbing the towel all over her, touching her in all the right places . . .

Yeah, dream on, silly lady. That would never happen in this life time. Miguel had said he'd already picked out someone he wanted to have a serious relationship with. But why didn't he bring this lady to the salsa club, instead of her and Lisa? Maybe because the woman didn't dance. Or maybe he liked teaching salsa to a couple of newbies like she and Lisa. And he took them to the club so they could experience the real thing.

There were any number of reasons. But what was the real one? He was such an enigma. But a sexy, wonderful enigma, who could send her flying off beyond the stars simply by looking at her with those gorgeous, soft brown eyes of his.

Marita gave her hair a vigorous rub to banish such thoughts. She had no business flying off beyond the stars.

Maybe having dinner with Steve was just the ticket to cure her of this nonsense.

The restaurant was full when Marita entered. She hoped she'd be able to recognize Steve after only having met him once in the dimly lit dance hall. Yes, there he was, standing and waving to her. He came to meet her at the door, took her by the shoulders and kissed her on both the cheeks.

"Hello, Marita."

Thank goodness it was just on the cheeks because after the searing kiss with Miguel at the last dance, Marita didn't want any other lips touching hers. She brought her fingertips up to touch her lips, which tingled at the mere thought of Miguel's mouth on them. The earth had turned on its axis and changed everything for her in those fleeting moments. So what was she doing here, meeting Steve for dinner tonight? Was she crazy?

She smiled sweetly. "Hello, Steve."

No, she wasn't crazy. She just didn't want life to pass her by, while Miguel danced off with another Jessica. The way Ron had done. Except Miguel wouldn't be leaving her, since there was nothing for him to leave from. Marita would be just sitting there, with no "Left Behind" sign on her forehead. Being left behind by Miguel would have been a thousand times worse than being left behind by Ron, so it was good it wasn't ever going to happen. Whew!

Steve pulled out a chair for her. "I hope you don't mind that I already ordered the wine. White." There was a bottle on the table, and the glasses were poured.

Marita didn't need to peruse the menu. This restaurant was one where she came often, so she almost knew the selection by heart.

"If you like fish and chips, I would highly

recommend that," she said. "That's their specialty."

"Gosh, I hope you don't mind, Marita, but I try to keep away from French fries," Steve said. "I'm a bit on the heavy side, as you can see, so—"

"Steve you look perfectly fine to me." If he was so weight conscious, what was he doing here with her?

Steve's face lit up. "You think so?"

"Yes, I do. You look good."

"Well, in that case I'll take the fish and chips if you recommend them so highly," he announced cheerfully. "I do a lot of salsa to keep my weight in check. Middle-age spread, you know."

Marita nodded. "I'm afraid I'm only too familiar with it." Middle age. That was something they unarguably had in common. Though it would have been nicer if they had both collected stamps.

Steve relaxed back in his chair. "Hey, let's drink to what we both like. Good food and salsa." He held up his glass and Marita saluted him with hers.

The food arrived and Steve picked up a French fry with his fingers. "You are right. This is excellent." He began to eat with obvious relish.

Marita broke off a piece of breaded halibut. "I'm glad you like it. As you may have noticed, lots of people here are eating this."

Steve popped another fry into his mouth. "Now that you've met me and seen how harmless I am, would you consider going out with me? To the theatre, perhaps? Maybe a concert?"

If he'd have asked her to a basketball game, or a roller derby, or some other sports event in which she had absolutely no interest, her answer would have been an immediate and emphatic negative. But a concert? Why not? What did she have to lose except an evening at home by herself? These days Lisa was either in class or out socializing with her new-found school friends. Or at some classmate's home working on a project. Which was what she told Marita, anyway.

"A concert sounds good," she said to Steve. "Did you have something in mind?"

"I have two tickets to a concert of Argentinean music and dance this Saturday. I bought them in hopes of being able to entice you to come with me."

Really? Buying two expensive theatre tickets after just one dance and one phone conversation with her? He'd probably bought them in hopes of finding someone—anyone—to go with him. Or maybe someone had stood him up? But whatever was the reason he had them, she decided to accept his invitation.

Steve looked like he'd struck gold. "And I'm also looking forward to dancing with you at the club tomorrow night."

"Yes, that'll be fun." Well, at least it had been the last time they danced.

Marita took the bus home, having rejected Steve's offer to drive her. She smiled to herself as she thought of Steve telling her how much he'd enjoyed the fish and chips. He'd wolfed them down like a starving man, proving it wasn't wise to keep away too long from something you lusted after. Like French fries. Or sex.

After three years of no nooky—and not much for quite some time before that—Marita had to admit her appetite for sex was building up. Maybe she didn't need to cast her nets out beyond Steve. He seemed like a nice enough guy. But could she imagine herself standing stark naked in front of him? No way, José! Even though he, himself, sported a nice pair of love-handles, he was definitely too weight-conscious. How would he react to a woman with a back-side that resembled a pair of potato sacks?

Chapter Six

Miguel came to pick Marita up on Friday night for their dance date at the Spadina Salsa Club. She tried to think of it as her exercise class, kind of like last fall's art classes, where the handsome teacher, Michael Merrick, had provided a bit of sexual titillation to his pupils. So now was she also simply looking for some thrills, going to these dances with Miguel?

Art lessons, dance lessons, was there really any difference? Oh yeah. Salsa classes gave her much more than the art classes had, because she got to dance in a sexy way with her teacher. In fact, she could almost say she got to make love with him. Standing up. With their clothes on. With plenty of foreplay. And when the person you danced with was the one you were crazy about, it was hugely intoxicating stuff. But when the one you were crazy about danced like that with every other woman, including his ex, and had no idea you were swooning all over him, that hurt.

Obviously Steve had been waiting for them, because almost the minute they were seated he came up.

"Hello, Marita, I'm so glad you came," he said

enthusiastically. "I hope your dance teacher won't mind if I grab you for a few numbers tonight."

The look Miguel shot at Steve was far from inviting. "I'm afraid we've been working on some new steps and I'd prefer—"

"But Marita, last night at dinner you promised you'd dance with me," Steve said plaintively.

Miguel's questioning frown made Marita gulp. Did Miguel object to her having had dinner with Steve? Was he jealous? The thought made her heart take a few joyous skips, but his next words set it back on its heels.

"Well, in that case I guess you'd better keep your word." With a nod to Steve, Miguel rose and walked off, leaving Marita staring miserably after him. What exactly had just happened?

Steve sat down in Miguel's chair and smiled at her. "I've been looking forward to dancing with you since last week," he said, taking her hand in his.

"Right." Through unfocused eyes Marita saw Miguel on the dance floor with Jessica. And she couldn't stop looking at them even though they swayed and bucked their hips in a way that left nothing to imagination. They were probably reliving the sex they'd enjoyed as a couple. Or maybe they had patched up their differences and were still a couple. What, after all, did she know about Miguel?

Yes, what did she know about Miguel except he liked salsa and was an artist who gave art classes each week to a bunch of adoring women? She remembered how his partner, Michael, had taken advantage of these fawning students to provide himself with some "amusement", until Shaylee had come along and captured his heart.

Maybe Miguel was doing the same? And why not? He was a bachelor and not in a romantic relationship with anyone. Or was he? Hadn't he told her he had found someone for a more meaningful relationship? It didn't seem that someone was Lisa, so could it be Jessica after all?

Marita shook her head. She felt like a teen-ager mulling over the romantic relationships of her high school BFFs. Enough, already. She'd come here to dance for exercise, and not for any other reason. And especially not to ponder about other people's sex lives.

She turned to Steve. "So, shall we dance?"

"Absolutely." He pulled her to her feet. "Let's boogie." His arm went around her waist and his hips began to sway.

Marita tried to enjoy the dance like she had the previous week, but somehow tonight it didn't feel the same. Every few minutes she caught sight of Miguel and Jessica rubbing against each other. That hurt.

"I'm sorry. Please excuse me, Steve, but I have a terrible head ache." She tore herself free, went to pick up her purse, and walked quickly to the ladies' room.

In a cubicle she leaned her forehead against the cool stainless steel partition and took some deep breaths, striving to calm herself and steady her pounding heart. No, dammit! She did not want Miguel's arms around Jessica.

After a few minutes she emerged and walked back to the table where Steve was waiting patiently.

"Sorry, Steve," Marita said as soon as she sat down. "But I can't dance right now. I took a headache tablet so I'm sure I'll be fine in a few minutes. But you might as well go and pick yourself another partner. No use you spoiling your evening, too."

Steve left reluctantly, but soon she saw him on the floor with a young lady wearing a slinky skirt with tassels on the hem. They danced well, and Steve looked perfectly happy, which made Marita feel less guilty.

And Miguel didn't look too sad either. He and Jessica were throbbing along like a house on fire. Marita wanted to leave and go home by herself, but the idea of making a scene was distasteful, so she stayed put.

"W-hell," she breathed when Miguel finally returned to the table. "That was some hot dancing." She rolled her eyes and forced her voice to sound like she considered the whole thing extremely amusing.

Miguel sat down. "Where's Steve?" he asked.

"He's dancing, I believe." Marita looked around the dance floor as if to check. "Yup. There he is. He's really smokin', too."

"Marita," Miguel snapped. "What exactly is going on with you and this Steve? He said you two went out for dinner and—"

"Exactly? You sure you want all the sordid details?" Although she said it lightly, she knew Miguel heard the sarcasm in her voice because anger flashed in his dark eyes.

"Yes," he said sharply.

"Well . . ." Marita slowly held up one finger. "We went out for dinner and . . ." She uncurled another finger. "He asked if he could dance with me tonight." Another finger went up. "And he invited me to an Argentinean concert. Yup. That's about it."

A look of surprise swept across Miguel's face, erasing the frown. "An Argentinean concert? When?"

This sudden curiosity surprised her, to say the

least. "Tomorrow night. Why do you ask?"

"I'm going to that concert, too," he exclaimed. "What a coincidence."

"Yes, isn't it, though." With whom was he going? More than likely not alone. But she was not going to ask. No way, José! It was absolutely no business of hers.

With a mischievous smile Miguel said, "I'm going with a very lovely lady," he said. "I hope I can introduce her to you at the concert."

"Right. Let's hope." Did he have to rub it in her face, damn him?

They left shortly after, because Marita's "headache" didn't seem to get any better. On the way home there was no talk of Steve, or of the concert where Miguel would be with some lovely lady.

But in Marita's head a real headache was beginning to develop.

They parted with a quick kiss on the lips. Those breathtaking words and that incredible, searing kiss only a few days ago now seemed like a dream that had never happened.

Bah! Who cared about such silly nonsense. It meant absolutely nothing!

The foyer of the Elgin Theatre was packed, and although Marita tried to locate Miguel, she couldn't see him in the crowd that was streaming in.

She and Steve were seated up on the balcony, which gave her an excellent view of the audience below. It took some searching but at last she saw Miguel, sitting beside—just as he'd told her—a lovely lady. It wasn't Jessica. And obviously not his mother.

The lights dimmed and the show started. Clacking

her castanets, a señorita in a tight red gown stepped smartly out into the spotlight. She flung the long train of her skirt around as she tapped her way through a fiery flamenco. It was all very exciting, but Marita had trouble concentrating on the performance. Her mind was preoccupied with Miguel and his lovely lady below.

During intermission Steve led her to the lobby where he had pre-ordered two glasses of wine. As they sipped their drinks, Marita again tried to locate Miguel.

All at once Steve raised his arm and waved excitedly. "Hey, there's your dance instructor. What's his name again?"

"Miguel."

"Right. He's got a very lovely companion," Steve commented. He had obviously caught Miguel's eye because he was waving them over.

Marita wanted to shrink into a tiny ball. She did not want to be introduced to the lovely lady. She had only wanted to see her out of curiosity, not talk to her.

But soon Miguel and his date approached them.

"This is Marita Osborne whom I've told you about," Miguel said to the lady. "And this is Marita's good friend, Steve—I'm sorry, I've forgotten your last name."

"Applebaum," Steve told him. "Steve Applebaum."

"Hello, Steve," the lovely lady said. "I'm Angela Cordova, Miguel's sister."

Marita's jaw dropped and simultaneously her mood lifted. In fact it soared right up to the crystal chandeliers high above on the domed, gilded ceiling.

"Glad to meet you, Angela," she said and a genuine smile replaced her pasted-on one.

"Marita, I wanted to ask you to come with me to this concert, but I'd already invited my sister and purchased the tickets long ago. It's her birthday present," Miguel explained. "But since you already had a date with Steve, it was just as well," he added, and Marita thought she detected a sharp edge to his voice.

Nah. No edge, only wishful thinking on her part.

Angela laughed. "I'm sure Miguel would much rather have spent the evening in your company, Marita. He's told me so much about you."

He had? Such as what? Marita was burning with curiosity but instead she said, "Well, I'm afraid he's not been as communicative about his family. I'm sorry to say he's never even mentioned that he had a sister."

Angela turned to Miguel and tapped him on the arm with her program. "That's terrible. Marita might get the impression you don't love your family."

Miguel pulled his sister into the crook of his arm. "Ah, but you know I do, my sweet little sister."

"Well, I'm going to tattle to mother you've not told Marita about us," Angela threatened.

"We've been too busy talking about other things," Miguel protested.

"Such as?" Angela pursued with a twinkle in her eyes, but just then the first warning bell rang.

Steve had finished his wine and took Marita by the arm. "Drink up, dear. Time to get back to enjoy the show."

Marita handed him the half-full glass. "Thanks, Steve, but I don't want to chug it down. Could you take it to the bar, please."

She turned to Angela. "It's been very nice meeting you." If only Angela knew how nice.

"Yes, I'm sure we'll meet again soon," Angela said.

"Listen, Marita," Miguel broke in. "Do you think you and Steve would like to come with us after the show for a nightcap?" He took her hand. "Please?"

"I think Steve would agree to that," Marita said, a blush rising to her cheeks. He sure didn't need to twist her arm too hard to get her to agree. Miguel gave her hand a gentle squeeze and a warm glow spread through her.

"I'm glad," he said and flashed her a smile before surrendering her hand. "We'll meet here in the lobby."

Steve appeared behind Marita. "There goes the second warning bell," he said. "We better start climbing up to the nose-bleed section."

Before the lights went out, Marita saw Miguel turn to scan the balcony. When he located her, he smiled and gave her a little wave.

The second half of the show was definitely much more delightful than the first.

As they made their way down after the show, Steve asked, "Will you come with me to the dance on Friday? I think you dance fine and don't need your instructor around any more."

"Thank you, Steve," Marita said. His acknowledgement certainly spread soothing balm on her self-esteem, but she couldn't even think of not being in Miguel's arms. "But Miguel thinks I still have a lot to learn, so we'll keep dancing together for the time being. He frowns on me dancing with other men who might confuse me." Balderdash! She just wanted to discourage Steve's advances without being rude.

"But you know I'm a great leader. You're never confused with me."

He was right, of course, and Marita didn't know how to extricate herself from this. She was happy to see Angela waving to them among the lobby crowds.

With them stood another man—a tall, blond fellow, who was chatting with Miguel.

"Marita, guess who we ran into?" Miguel said. "This is Mika, the third Michael in our business. I happened to catch him as he was going out, and he's agreed to come for a drink with us."

As Mika looked her over, Marita was sure she saw a look of surprise in his eyes.

"So you're Marita," Mika said. Yes, definitely it had been a look of surprise. Obviously the real live Marita didn't match with whatever picture Miguel had painted of her.

"Miguel's been telling me a lot about you lately." Mika went on.

Not him, too! Marita was dying to know what stories Miguel had been spreading about her, but for once she bit her tongue. "I hope it's been good?" There was something about Mika's reaction that made her feel self-conscious and uncomfortable.

"They have indeed."

Steve stepped up and put a possessive arm around Marita's shoulders. "Well," he said with a forced laugh. "Looks like Miguel has been telling everybody about my date. His sister. His friend. I'm almost beginning to think he's more than just a dance instructor."

Marita could sense his confusion and hurried to explain. "Actually, Steve, Miguel is, or used to be, my art teacher. And then he became my dance instructor when I wanted to learn the salsa."

"I see." Steve nodded but didn't look convinced.

"That's it. There is no more," Marita assured him. Because that's all there was. Period.

"So, are you a fan of Argentinean music?" Marita asked Mika when they were settled at a round table in a nearby restaurant. She sat on one side of Mika and Angela sat on the other. That put Miguel across the table, much too far away.

"Not particularly," Mika replied. "But Miguel obviously is. He told me about this show some time ago and I thought I'd come and see what he was raving about."

"Great, wasn't it?" Steve put in, leaning forward past Marita to speak to Mika. "I'm a great fan of all things Latin. You must be Anglo-Saxon, being so blond."

"Actually, I'm a Finn," Mika told him. "My grandparents came from Finland but my dad was born here. I'm planning to go to the old country in the near future. Finnish art interests me."

"I take it you fellows have all known each other for some time?" Steve asked.

"Since Art College," Miguel said. "After college Michael, Mika and I started our graphic design business and we've been together ever since."

Marita turned to Steve. "My friend, Shaylee, married Michael last summer. She comes from a large farming family near Kitchener."

"If Mika had been here, instead of traveling in Africa, he might have grabbed that Shaylee-cutie," Miguel said with a chuckle.

"Hey, you know I'm not into grabbing cuties for matrimonial purposes. That unavoidably leads to kids." Mika put an arm around Angela and pulled her close. "Besides, I've always been drawn to these dark, Latino types. Opposites attract, you know."

Angela removed his arm firmly. "But it takes two to tango," she said. "And I don't happen to be drawn to arrogant blond Finns."

Miguel reached across the table and took Marita's hand. "Well, something is drawing me over here."

Although, for Steve's sake, Marita should have

objected, she didn't.

Steve coughed. "I think I'm starting to feel like the fifth wheel. Even my girl is being claimed by someone else." He laughed to make light of the situation, but Marita could see a flash of annoyance in his eyes. Reluctantly she pulled her hand free and picked up her glass.

"A toast!" she cried. "To the total disarray of relationships at this table."

It was near midnight by the time Steve and Marita stood on the subway platform. By joking around, she'd managed to make Steve feel less like an uninvited guest and more like her date, even though Miguel's presence had made that difficult.

"I want to thank you for this evening, Steve," Marita said. "I had a great time." And that was true, especially after she'd discovered the woman with Miguel was his sister.

The almost empty train rumbled to the station, and the theatre crowd soon filled the seats. Steve and Marita ended up standing a few feet apart, holding onto the bar. That prevented any conversation for the rest of the trip, which suited Marita just fine. She didn't want to give Steve a chance to ask her to go dancing with him at the club the following week.

At her apartment door Steve looked down at the key in Marita's hand as though waiting for an invitation.

She pretended not to notice until he spoke up. "I guess it's too late for a cup of coffee?"

"My niece will be sleeping," Marita said and unlocked the door. She opened it only a crack, to indicate he wouldn't be coming in.

Steve's face fell. "Well, I'm hoping I'll see you Friday night at the club," he said and took her by the shoulders. Marita offered him her cheek and after his light kiss, she slipped inside with a quick, "Good night, Steve."

"I must say I was surprised when I saw Marita," Mika said, breaking the silence in the studio.

Miguel raised his head. "Oh? How come?"

Mika paused his computer, ready to discuss the issue. "Well, you know, she's not exactly your type."

Miguel frowned. "My type? What, in your learnèd opinion, is my type?"

"Don't get defensive. I'm not saying anything bad about the woman. I just mean she's not the kind you've usually associated and lived with. That's all. She's not the least bit like Jessica, for example. Or Emily before that. Or Georgia. You know what I mean."

"So what is it about Marita that surprises you?" Of course Miguel knew exactly what Mika was driving at but wanted to hear it from the horse's mouth. Marita was full-figured, unlike Jessica or the others Mika had named.

Mika looked embarrassed. "God, Miguel, do I have to spell it out? Usually you've gone for more, um, slender kind of women."

"That's true. What else?" He was making Mika squirm on purpose.

"Well, she's old-er. Probably over forty?"

"She's forty-three."

"And that doesn't bother you?"

"No. Why should it? But I can see it bothers you. And her. I'm trying to help her get over it by not ever saying anything about it."

"Okay. So, what it is about her that draws you?"

"She's . . ." What was it about Marita he loved?

"She's just right for me. She's feminine. I love to hold her when we dance. And I love to touch her." His hands moved, as though she were there before him. "She's soft and smooth and silky, with curves in all the right places. She's a real woman."

Mika laughed. "Oo-kay. I think I get it. And I stand corrected."

Miguel got up to pace the room. He wanted Mika to understand the attraction wasn't only physical. "I love her earthy laughter and her sense of humour. She really is something special. Listen, Mika, I had enough of Jessica's obsession with her weight. If an ounce of cellulite ever dared to creep up anywhere on her body, she went into hysterics. Taking her to a restaurant was a bore. God, not even a slice of birthday cake could pass her lips. Ever. A French fry? Forget it." Miguel snorted bitterly. "I couldn't take it any more, listening twenty-four seven to her obsess about her figure. Working to tone one part of her body or other with such and such an exercise routine."

"I'm sure all the women in your life weren't as bad as that. But okay, I can see where that might get a bit off-putting." Mika sounded empathetic.

"To me there's nothing sensuous about a woman like Jessica. I hate to say negative things about a beautiful woman, but since you brought it up . . . she started to turn me off. She's so shallow. And too hard. I mean her body. And even her nature, to some degree. She works out all the time and has a stomach like a washboard and that's all she talks about. Marita's so feminine. Funny. Thoughtful. Sexy. Softly-rounded—"

Mika hooted. "Pal, you make her sound delicious."

"She is."

"Do you realize, you're getting all dewy-eyed talking

about her?"

"And for a good reason."

"But you must admit, Jessica does look great in a bikini." Mika wagged his eyebrows lecherously.

"Sure, if you like hard, sinewy bodies."

Mika sighed. "I give up. You're hopeless." He turned and settled back to work.

Miguel returned to his table and for a while he was silent as he tapped his pencil on the desk. He'd been thinking about an idea for some time. Maybe as far back as last spring when he met Marita in the art class. He wanted to pass it by Mika and get his take on it.

"I'm thinking of asking Marita to model for me," he finally said. "I find her curves and her soft lines quite inspiring. What do you think?"

Immediately Mika looked interested. "Yeah, you do like to paint curves. Even in landscapes you have a kind of curvaceous tendency."

"That's what I was thinking. I had an idea that maybe I'd combine female curves and the curves in nature. There are beautiful lines in both."

Mika nodded enthusiastically. "Yeah, I think you definitely should pursue that. You think she'll go for it?"

Miguel gave a mirthless laugh. "Go for it? Not in a million years. I think I'll be in for a slight struggle of wills, to put it mildly, but it's worth a try." He was aware of Marita's vulnerabilities and knew the struggle to convince her would be more than slight. Somehow he had to make her see how beautiful she was. And make her see that her age was not an issue between them.

"By the way, are you sure there are no other suitors vying for this prize catch?" Mika asked after a while.

"That Steve seemed very taken with her."

Miguel nodded. "As a matter of fact, there are others. I'll have to keep an eye on Steve, that old buzzard. He's been showing way too much interest in her. And her ex-husband has started to creep around her again for some reason. Maybe his marriage to a much younger woman is crumbling, or something."

Mika laughed uproariously. "Jeez, Miguel, you better put your dibs on her soon. You're starting to sound like some territorial buck fending off other males."

"I told you I'm taking it slow. I don't want to push her till I feel she's ready."

But he knew he couldn't wait much longer. It was getting harder and harder to stop himself from carrying her off to the bedroom, after dancing with her in her apartment.

Miguel threw his jacket on the back of a red kitchen chair. "Where's Lisa tonight?"

It was lesson night and Marita had already rolled up the rug to transform the apartment into a dance floor.

"She's gone to her girlfriend's for the night. They're working on some project together," she told him as she came up to greet him.

He put his arms around her and kissed her as usual. "A likely story. She's probably staying the night with her boyfriend."

"Miguel!" Marita cried. "That's not so. Lisa hasn't got a regular boyfriend yet. And even if she did, she wouldn't—"

"Wouldn't she? Are you sure?" He gazed at her and the hunger inside him grew as he held her in his arms.

He could hear Marita's breath catch in her throat.

"Well, if she did, it wouldn't be any of my business," she murmured.

"That's right." Miguel rested his forehead against hers. "And what we do when she's not here is not her business."

He pressed her against him and slid his palms along her smooth, luscious curves. And then his lips were on hers again, but this time they stayed, hot and demanding. "I want you," he whispered hoarsely.

She responded with equal hunger, moaning softly as her fingers dug into his back, pulling him closer. Still holding her in a kiss, Miguel slowly backed her into the bedroom. They fell onto the bed and he flipped her around on top of him. He'd been wanting so long to touch her. Every part of her. To feel her silky skin against his body with no clothes to spoil the sensation. To bury himself into her.

Marita held herself up with her arms while he unbuttoned her blouse. Her eyes were wide with a fierce, naked yearning that told him she wanted him. Unabashedly wanted him. This knowledge made him harden even more. Almost crazed with desire, his impatient fingers unclasped her bra and allowed her lush breasts to fall into his waiting hands. With a groan of satisfaction he kissed them hungrily and buried his face in their fullness.

"You're beautiful," he breathed.

"Mmm," she responded, smiling her pleasure, and arched her back to give him more of what he lusted for.

She turned over to lie on her back while he unzipped her short, figure-hugging skirt and peeled it off, along with her red panties, revealing her gently rounded, feminine belly.

Marita moved her hips sensuously, impatiently, showing her readiness and eagerness. "Please say you brought a condom."

He had, and as soon as he had divested himself of his own clothing, he sheathed himself and returned to cover her with his body.

Their lovemaking was mutually frantic and every fibre of his body responded to her passionate, abandoned demands. She was wonderfully free and tempestuous and held nothing back.

When it was over they lay, damp and exhausted on the rumpled bed, steeped in satisfaction.

"Well, Mr. Cordova," Marita said stretching deliciously. "I must say you did yourself proud."

"Thanks. I can't say I was disappointed, either." Lying beside her, Miguel reached down to dab her stomach with little kisses. "My favourite place," he said. "Right after these." He fondled her breasts. "And this." His hand moved down to her mound.

"And what about my luscious lips?" Marita demanded puckering up.

Miguel laughed and took her pouty lips into his mouth, sucking them gently. "Definitely there on the top of the list, along with the rest of you," he said after he released her. "You're a perfect package."

Marita smiled dreamily. "As are you, my Latin lover."

Was this really happening to her? It had to be a dream, because there was no way Miguel could be here, in her bed, making passionate love to her. She pinched him.

"Ow!" he yowled. "What was that for?"

"I wanted to see if you were real. I thought maybe I

was dreaming you were here in my bed, making wild love to me."

"I'm here. And next time, please just ask me, and I'll tell you if I'm here in body or only in your mind."

Next time? Was there going to be a next time? Please God, let him mean that.

"Is there going to be a next time?" Her voice was almost inaudible.

Miguel gazed down at her, his eyes filled with tenderness. "I sure hope so," he murmured and kissed her so deeply and completely it erased all doubt from her mind.

When he raised his head she saw desire again reflected in his dark pupils. This made all the blood in her body plummet down to boil in her groin area. She had trouble getting her lungs to do their normal routine for what was happening here tonight was beyond wonderful.

"Marita, I think I'm falling for you," he said, and her heart gave an impossibly huge leap of joy.

But for her there was no "I think". She knew she was desperately in love with him. Of course it was only the sex that was making him say those wonderful words, but . . . why was he talking like this when there was someone else on his mind? A woman he'd found for a meaningful relationship.

She swallowed hard before asking. "Remember when you told me you were looking for a more meaningful relationship?"

"Yes," he replied, lazily playing with one of her nipples.

"Well?"

"I've definitely found her," he said with a salacious smile. "As long as you're willing to go along with it, of course."

"Me?" Happiness pushed away any doubts about his intentions. Miguel wanted to have a "meaningful relationship" with her! That meant no other women—at least not for the time being—existed in his life. And that was good enough for her. She would be an absolute fool to deny herself this delicious pleasure, even if it was only for the time being.

"Of course you, silly girl," Miguel said with a laugh. "Do you think I'd be making love to you if there was someone else on deck?" He tapped her nose with his finger. "What kind of a gigolo do you think I am?"

"I think you're wonderful, whatever you are," Marita exclaimed and swung herself on top of him, straddling his stomach. She took his face into her hands and kissed him, feeling him harden beneath her.

"This time we'll take it slow and easy," he said and pulled her down so he could bury his face between her breasts. "I want to taste you and savour you to the fullest."

There was a loud knock on the door.

Chapter Seven

"What the bloody hell!" Miguel exploded. "Are you expecting someone? The landlord? The plumber?"

"No one," Marita said, half-rising. Who could it be?

Miguel pulled her back down and gently pecked at one nipple with his teeth. "Leave it, then," he murmured from the corner of his mouth.

"I can't. It could be important. Maybe something about Lisa." Reluctantly she got up and grabbed her housecoat from the floor.

She went to the door and peered through the peephole. Ron was standing in the hallway. Marita opened the door a crack.

"What are you doing here, Ron?" She spoke loudly enough for Miguel to hear. "It's past nine. Way past dinner time."

Ron pushed himself in. "Some kind soul let me in as I was standing there, ready to press your code," he told her.

"How very kind of him."

"Her."

"Whatever. So why are you here?" She stood her ground to prevent him from coming in any further.

"I was just passing by and thought I'd come and spend the evening with you, in case you were lonely."

"That was very thoughtful of you, Ron. But Lisa lives here, too, remember? She keeps me company."

"I know, but sometimes some masculine company might be nice for a change." His voice had an undisguised suggestive tone and he nudged himself further into the hall.

Marita couldn't help it. She burst into a loud guffaw. "And you thought you'd come and provide me with that?"

Ron looked hurt. "I was only trying to be friendly," he said. He finally noticed her housecoat. "You weren't going to bed already, were you?"

Again Marita laughed. "As a matter of fact I was in bed already."

At that moment Miguel appeared at the bedroom door. He was casually doing up a button on his white shirt which was open, revealing his smooth, bronzed chest. His bare feet and the undone belt told the story.

Ron's jaw dropped. "Oh, it's you," he finally managed to croak. "The dance teacher."

"No," Miguel said calmly, and did up a couple more buttons. "A very close friend." The meaningful emphasis he put on the word "close" sent a pleasant shiver of warmth through Marita from her scalp down to her bare toes. She felt wonderfully wanted.

But at this moment there was one "wanter" too many in the room. Miguel must have felt the same, because he came forward and stood in front of Ron.

"Marita and I were busy," he said and his tone left nothing to imagination. Ron would've had to be a total dunce not to get the message.

Miguel pushed the door open. "Do you mind?"

After Ron had slunk out, looking embarrassed and confused, Miguel turned to Marita and undid the belt of her housecoat.

"Why do you let him come here?" He slipped the housecoat off her shoulders and slid his hands down along her hourglass curves. "I thought a divorce means it's over." He bent down, his lips following his hands, rousing her desire as they progressed down her body. "Like completely over."

"Of course it's over," she managed to croak as her breath abandoned her lungs. "It's been over for three years." His lips kept sliding down, sprinkling little kisses on their way.

"With all these Steves and Rons hankering after you, pretty soon I'm going to have to take a number and get in line." His voice turned darker as he sunk to his knees, savouring her.

"Never," Marita breathed. "You'll always be my number one." She dug her fingers into his black hair and closed her eyes in ecstasy.

"And make sure it stays that way," Miguel growled. His lips and hands had reached their goal. Grasping her buttocks, he kissed her intimately where no man had ever kissed her before.

Marita could feel his tongue move, and she arched her body, opening herself up for him. She pulled his head against her, afraid he would stop, and her breath came in quick gasps. This was something so primitive, so intense, but so right. She quickly climaxed and he gently lowered her to the floor as her legs buckled under her. When he kissed her, she could taste herself on his lips.

"And now back to business. We weren't finished, remember? The carpet or the bed?"

An hour later they lay in bed, mellow and satisfied after their languorous love making. Marita looked at Miguel, stretched out beside her, totally relaxed, naked and beautiful. If only this could continue for the rest of their lives. But, what the heck, since it wasn't in the cards she would take all the moments she could and never complain. It was definitely better than the lonely evenings by herself, with the odd unwanted visit from Ron.

Miguel rose on one elbow and brushed his fingers softly across her breasts, configuring the curves. "Darling," he said lazily. "I have a proposition to make."

"A proposition? You make me sound like a wanton woman," Marita murmured. "Which I am, of course."

"Only with me, I hope."

"Absolutely." She took his hand, put the middle finger into her mouth and sucked it. "So what were you going to propose?" she asked from the corner of her mouth. She knew it wasn't going to be marriage. Too bad, so sad.

"I'd like you to model for me."

She could feel him holding his breath.

"In the nude." He let out his breath and waited.

Marita popped his finger out of her mouth and sat bolt upright. "Miguel, are you crazy? I don't do modeling. Not with clothes on, not nude. No way José!"

"I wanted to try something I've been thinking about for a while," Miguel continued, ignoring her denial. He sat up and looked at her earnestly. "I want to paint a woman's beautiful curves reflected against the curves found in nature."

"And I guess for that you need someone with lots of curves?" She gave a little forced laugh. "Finally a valid reason for voluptuosity."

"Darling, you're absolutely ideal."

"Yeah, right." She hopped out of bed and reached for her housecoat. "Forget it."

But he pulled her back down beside him and began to nuzzle her neck, sending delicious shivers down her body. "You don't know how simply looking at you inspires me. We'd be at my atelier in my condo. Just the two of us. What do you say?"

"I say you are one crazy nut!"

"Afterward, we could . . ."

His hands wandered over her body and she felt him harden as he deliberately pressed himself against her.

"This is blackmail," she complained, breathless.

"No, it's bribery," he murmured and placed her hand where she could feel the full, hard length.

"You think I'm an easy mark," she groaned. "Doing it just for the thrill of sex."

"I was hoping as much."

"When do we start?"

Miguel laughed triumphantly and covered her again with his body. "Next week."

"I feel pretty! I feel pretty!" Marita sang and danced around the apartment. Miguel wanted her for a meaningful relationship. Wow! That was almost as good as him saying he was falling in love with her. Of course it wasn't in the same league at all, but he had called her beautiful—ideal even.

She stopped in front of the hall mirror. "Who can that lovely girl in the mirror be?" She sang and did another pirouette.

At that point Lisa opened the door and entered. "Whoa, Marita, what's going on?" She slipped the backpack off her shoulder and let it fall on the hall floor with a thump.

Marita did a few more turns. "I am dancing for joy!" she sang.

Lisa laughed. "And you're in love with a boy?"

Marita stopped dancing. "Well, maybe something like that."

Lisa picked up her backpack and headed for her room. "Mom'll be here in a few minutes," she announced. "We're going shopping for some winter clothes for me, and then we'll go for a bite to eat. You want to come along?"

"No, thanks," Marita called. "I'm working on a menu for a huge birthday party for some millionaire. I have to come up with some pretty spectacular food ideas."

Lisa came out, slipping a casual t-shirt over her head. "So that's why you were dancing all over the apartment? Drumming up some inspiration?"

The phone rang, and shortly after Rosalyn bustled in. She immediately flopped into an armchair. "The traffic is awful," she announced.

"I'm fine, thanks. And how are you, Rosalyn?" Marita said.

"Mom, did you know Marita's in love?" Lisa blurted out.

Marita bit her lip and strongly considered tossing her niece over the balcony railing. "I don't believe I said anything about being in love, Lisa." Although the girl was right, of course. She was. Madly and deeply in love.

"Yes, but the way you were dancing and singing just now, it's obvious."

Rosalyn perked up. "That's very nice, Martha," she said. "It's about time you found yourself a man."

"A man? Oh, Mom, Marita has men coming out of

her ears," Lisa warbled. "Even Uncle Ron has started lurking around here. Especially at dinner time," she added with a giggle.

Rosalyn sat up straight to discuss the matter more closely. "Ron? But I thought the woman he married was young and beautiful and perfect. Why would he be coming back to his old wife?"

Marita pursed her lips. That was Rosalyn, all right. It was no use getting her knickers in a knot over things her sister spat out. "I guess the old wife can still be a hot item. Especially when it comes to food," she said.

"Of course I meant 'former', when I said 'old'," Rosalyn corrected herself tartly. "No need to get sarcastic."

"Thank you, Rosalyn. Makes me feel ever so much better."

"And then there's Steve, who's a great salsa dancer," Lisa went on. "They went out for dinner and to the theatre. And he wants Marita to go out with him more often, but she won't."

Obviously big-eared Lisa had overheard some phone conversations.

"Why on earth not?" Rosalyn wanted to know. "Especially if he's such a good dancer. You always liked dancing. I remember you and Ron often went—"

"It's because of Miguel," Lisa interrupted her mother with her big news. "Marita, you were dancing and singing because of Miguel, weren't you? Come on, fess up," she teased, laughing.

Marita retreated into the kitchen to take a few deep breaths. She absolutely did not want to create a scene in front of Rosalyn.

"So, tell me about this Miguel," Rosalyn said, following Marita into the kitchen. "What's he like?"

"He's an artist," Marita told her." A very nice young man."

Marita could almost see Rosalyn's ears waggle. "Young? What do you mean by young?"

"Oh, he's about thirty-three, I guess," Marita replied casually. "Give or take a year or two." She moved the butter dish on the counter. And then moved it back again to the same place.

"And you're forty-three, Martha," Rosalyn reminded her.

As if that fact wasn't always uppermost in Marita's mind these days. "And I'll be forty-four in November. Don't forget to send me a birthday card."

"He also dances salsa," Lisa piped up from the living room. "He comes here to teach Marita, and if I'm home he teaches me, too." Lisa entered the kitchen swaying and bucking her hips suggestively. "He is one hot guy."

"Stop that, young lady," Rosalyn said angrily. "I don't want you to dance those kinds of dances. Martha, how could you let Lisa learn dances like that?"

"Aw, Mom, we're both doing it for exercise," Lisa said. "Here, I have a video I took of Marita and Miguel dancing the other night." She ran into her room and emerged with her tablet.

"Lisa, I don't think you should—" Marita began but it was too late. Rosalyn was already looking at the video and Marita could swear her sister's eyes actually grew bigger.

"My word," Rosalyn gasped. "That is simply obscene. And this Miguel looks like he's a mere lad. It's absolutely not appropriate for a person your age to be gyrating like that with someone young enough to be your son."

Marita's jubilant mood had already evaporated, and

at this point it came close to crashing to the floor.

"For God's sake, Rosalyn. It's only a ten-year difference. Why are you making such an issue of that? And we're only dancing, not getting married or something." Yeah, maybe they weren't getting married, but certainly they were doing "something".

"Because it's indecent, that's why. At your age, you should know better."

Marita exploded. "If I want to go out with a man who is ten years younger, I'll damn well go out with a man who is ten years younger. Or twenty years younger if I feel like it!"

So much for holding her temper.

Rosalyn gasped. "So now you're going with this Miguel, are you? Not only taking lessons from him, but actually dating him? Oh God, people will say my sister is a cougar!"

"Mom!" Lisa cried. "You can't say that about Marita. That's cruel."

"Martha needs to know how the world is going to view her if she continues," Rosalyn said severely.

"My name is not Martha," Marita hissed. "It's Marita. And I would appreciate it if you'd start to remember that." She had to get out of here before she threw something, or said something unforgivable.

She made a dash for her bedroom. "And I'm going to model for him," she threw defiantly over her shoulder. "In the nude!" She made sure the door slammed hard enough for Rosalyn to know it wasn't safe to enter.

After Lisa and Rosalyn left, Marita made herself a cup of tea and then sat down on the couch, trying to calm down. Was she furious with Rosalyn for spoiling her jubilant, happy mood? Or for telling her the truth?

Fact was, she was a cougar. And it was totally indecent for her to be having sex with Miguel.

Wild and wonderful sex. After which she always felt better than ever in her entire life. Young. Vibrant. Beautiful. Wanted. And even loved, although he hadn't actually said that. But what the heck, young, vibrant, beautiful and wanted were enough.

Defiantly Marita straightened her shoulders and took a sip of the tea that was cooling fast. Why shouldn't she simply enjoy this? Yes, she'd once told herself she didn't want to be his hanky-panky provider between girlfriends but, dammit all, life was passing her by.

When a silver platter was handed to her with a gloriously hot red rose on it, why shouldn't she take it? How many opportunities would come up for her to enjoy great sex with a man she loved? Miguel obviously liked having sex with her. And he was a great lover. So why shouldn't she go for it? She might as well enjoy this wild ride while it lasted and let the devil take tomorrow.

"Let the devil take tomorrow". Marita winced as she thought back to the first time she and Miguel had danced the tango and he had sung Kiss of Fire. Would that end up as her theme song? So be it. Nothing wrong with that. She got up to bring the cup into the kitchen and took a few tango steps on the way.

"Give me your lips, the lips you only let me borrow," she sang and hugged herself. "Love me, Miguel, and let the devil take tomorrow."

The demanding birthday menu kept Marita busy every evening that week. She sat in the living room with her cookbooks and brochures scattered on the coffee table and on the couch beside her.

"Some people have way too much money to throw around," she complained to Lisa. "Such a big fuss over a child's eleventh birthday. If it were some important milestone, like the fiftieth, I could understand, but—"

"Maybe the child is sick and will never see her twelfth birthday," Lisa opined from the kitchen where she had commandeered the table for her school work.

"Sure, make me feel totally awful," Marita exploded. "Now I'll be thinking of this sweet child on her deathbed, instead of complaining about her having an overblown birthday party. Thanks a lot."

She was already feeling sorry for herself because she'd had to cancel the salsa lesson this week, depriving her of a chance to be with Miguel. She yearned for him with the thirst of someone crawling on a parched desert. This intense longing for him—and for sex—had taken her by surprise. Having had a taste of this delight after so many years, and enjoying it like she never had with Ron, she couldn't stop thinking about sex. And Miguel. Even at work, every so often she had to jolt herself out of daydreams filled with sex. And Miguel.

But Friday night was coming and she would once again be in his arms at the club. Lisa had already said she couldn't make it because of the upcoming midterms, so Miguel would be all hers. Not that she ever begrudged Lisa a few dances with him.

Of course Steve would be there, too. In fact he'd called a couple of times during the week to ask how she was and if she was coming to the club on Friday night. He hadn't asked directly if she would accompany him as his date, but had said he couldn't wait to dance with her. She had cut short the conversations, using her work as an excuse, because she didn't want to lead Steve on. She didn't think the phone was the proper medium for telling him about her emotional commitment to Miguel. She wanted to do it face to face.

Miguel, on the other hand, had called only once to find out how her work was coming along and then had left her alone to concentrate on her assignment. She knew he was being considerate, and he had his art class to teach and his own art projects to work on, but still she wished he'd have been less thoughtful and not quite so considerate. To hear his voice would have been like spreading soothing salve on a throbbing wound.

As soon as Marita and Miguel entered the club on Friday night and had settled down at their table, Steve popped up. Marita was still reeling from the passionate kisses Miguel had given her when he came to pick her up. Her fevered response had told him how much she'd missed him, too. They would have fallen right into bed but Lisa was home, busily studying, preventing them from going any further.

"Hi, Marita. Miguel," Steve said cheerfully and leaned both hands against the back of an empty chair. "Glad you could make it." He seemed to be waiting for an invitation to sit down. After standing there, chatting about the weather, he at last understood an invitation wasn't forthcoming. "Make sure you save me a dance, Marita," he said and went off to find himself another partner.

Marita couldn't help feeling bad about this too obvious dismissal, but as soon as she was in Miguel's arms she forgot all about Steve. After so many days of being without him, having him hold her again put her in smack dab the middle of Paradise.

At first they danced slowly, sensuously, even though the music tried its best to make them move faster. Marita only wanted to feel him against her, and from the way he held her tightly, she was sure he wanted the same. Tonight neither of them seemed to have any desire to boogie and twirl wildly.

"Darling, I've missed you so much," Miguel whispered in her ear. "I don't care how much work you have left to complete, tonight I want you all to myself."

"I've finished the project," Marita whispered, her throat constricted with desire. She wished they could be back in her apartment this very minute, making love, but Lisa was there, studying.

He slipped his leg between her thighs and she pressed herself against him, which only made her want him more.

"What if we leave early and go to my place?" Miguel suggested. "I don't have a niece studying there."

"What about a nephew?"

"Not one of those, either."

"Then—" she could barely croak, "what are we doing here?"

But as they returned to their table, Steve came over again.

"Marita, I think you could at least give me one dance," he said. "I want to talk to you."

Marita was thankful he was direct and, whatever was on his mind, he didn't hide it from Miguel. Without looking to see how Miguel was reacting, she simply nodded to Steve. "Of course. The next one is ours."

Miguel's face was a shade darker, but he said

nothing when the music started and she gave her hand to Steve.

"Let's boogie," Steve said, took a hold of her hands and twirled her around. It was easy to follow him.

"What did you want to say to me?" Marita asked when they were face to face again. Although, if it was what she suspected, she didn't want to hear.

"If we dance slower, maybe it'll be easier to talk," Steve said and took hold of her in a traditional manner, with his left hand behind her back. "Marita," he then began, looking earnestly into her eyes. "I want to be with you. I think about you all the time and would love nothing better than to be able to call you my girl."

Marita sighed. She'd been afraid of this, after the phone calls during the week. "Steve, I do like you," she began, "but I don't want to give you any false ideas. You're a nice guy, good-looking, a great dancer, and a fabulous catch for any woman. If I weren't involved with Miguel, I would be proud to be your girl. I really would. But I don't want to string you along because right now I want to be Miguel's girl."

They had stopped dancing and stood in the middle of the dance floor. Other couples had to slide past them, and occasionally gave them a bump.

"But surely you see that you and I would be a much better match," Steve said. "We're closer in age, and if we had a chance to develop our relationship, I'm sure we'd find we have much in common."

Yes, he was probably right. After all, what did she really know about Miguel? She had no idea if they had anything in common besides sex? And—she snorted— art. But he made her feel beautiful and loved and that was too precious a thing to simply toss away. Although one day it would be over, she wanted to hold onto it as long as possible. She counted herself among the lucky ones, for she knew too many people went through life never having experienced the joy she was feeling.

"I'm sorry, Steve." At least he didn't call her a cougar, like her own sister had done. For that alone she gave him a gold star.

Chapter Eight

Miguel frowned. Steve and Marita were dancing slowly. Too slowly. And too close. In fact they were just standing there. What the hell was going on?

It was a mistake to have come here. They should have driven straight to his condo, because every minute he was away from her he wanted her more. He wanted to hold her in his arms. To kiss her. To make love to her.

Enough of this. Miguel got up and walked over to where Marita and Steve were standing. He tapped Steve on the shoulder.

"Mind if I break in?" he asked and took Marita by the hand.

"No, of course not."

Steve looked somewhat dejected when he turned and walked away but Miguel didn't care. He led Marita to the coat check where he helped her with her overcoat.

"We're not dancing any more?" Marita asked. "Obviously."

"No," he replied and pulled on his black leather jacket.

Miguel's Corvette sped smartly down the dark city streets, but to him it took longer than forever before they reached his condo building down by the lake.

In the elevator going up to the twenty-seventh floor, Miguel slipped his hands inside her coat and pulled her against him.

"They have security cameras—" Marita began, but he brushed aside her concerns with a kiss.

At his door Miguel cursed as he searched for his key and finally located it in one of his pockets. The moment they were inside the condo, and the door was shut, he turned to her. Placing his palms against the wall, he claimed her with his mouth, kissing her hard, impatiently, possessively.

Marita clutched his shoulders for support as he began to disrobe her, still holding her only with his mouth. The coat fell to the floor, then the rest of her clothes in quick succession.

Marita fumbled with the buttons of his shirt and his belt buckle, whimpering impatiently, and soon his clothes joined hers on the floor.

Her nudity fired his passion and he groaned as they slid down onto the pile of coats, pants and underwear.

"Your condom," Marita whispered urgently.

"Damn." Miguel began to search for his wallet in the heap of clothes under them. He finally found it, pulled out the condom and ripped open the foil in a rush.

Their joining was frenzied, delirious, and spiked quickly.

"My God, I've waited for this all week," Miguel breathed. "I thought Friday would never come."

"I've missed you so much," was all she could say as she kissed his face again and again.

"Tomorrow is Saturday," Miguel said. "You don't

have to go home. In fact you can stay here all weekend."

Marita laughed. "If I do, I'll be too tired to work on Monday."

"Monday is Thanksgiving," Miguel reminded her and rose up from the impromptu bed. "No work for you."

She hooted. "On Tuesday I'll be a complete wreck if this was a sample of what's waiting for me here."

He watched her as she rose and, bending over, began to sort through their clothing. He loved the way her nicely-shaped derriere moved.

"We'll take the next round much more slowly and deliciously," Miguel assured her and couldn't keep himself from giving her bottom a loving stroke.

"Act two will take place on the bed," she announced. "Although I must admit making love on the hall floor atop a pile of coats and undies was an interesting experience."

"How about we try the kitchen table next?" Miguel asked.

"You serious? That's too hard. It's the bed or nothing, my Latin lover. I insist on some degree of comfort."

Miguel got up and sauntered with a sexy swagger toward the bedroom. He winked at Marita over his shoulder and crooked a finger, signaling for her to follow.

After more fabulous sex, Marita was ready to inspect the condo. Dressed in her pink silky panties and Miguel's blue pajama top, she wandered around, peeking into every room.

It was a modern, two-bedroom suite overlooking Lake Ontario. Miguel's atelier was in the second bedroom, which faced the lake, and had floor to ceiling windows covering the entire wall. A set of sliding doors led to a wide balcony.

"What a lovely view," Marita exclaimed. "I'm surprised you get any work done here. I would spend my whole day staring at that sparkling lake."

"I do my share of staring," Miguel confessed. "But I still get a lot of painting done. And speaking of painting—" He led her to a dais at the back wall of the studio.

Marita stopped in her tracks. "Hey, listen, I know I said I would do it, but I've been thinking. People are going to see me naked. That doesn't make me look like a good girl."

"Don't worry, darling. It's your body I'm after. Your face is beautiful, but for the art projects I only want your body." He pulled open the pajama top revealing her full breasts. "Your fabulous body."

Marita giggled and backed away. "So I'll be a headless woman sitting on a rock? Sounds kind of morbid. What kind of macabre art do you paint, anyhow?"

"I'll paint you a face but make it unrecognizable," Miguel told her. "Will that satisfy you?" He took her in his arms and nuzzled her neck, making her shiver with delight. "Please say yes?"

"Blow in my ear and I'll do anything you want," she murmured.

Miguel sucked on her earlobe. "People will admire your curves and no one but I will know who the luscious woman in the painting is." He picked her up in his arms and headed for the bedroom. "If you stay here for the weekend, we can start tomorrow morning."

Marita slipped quietly out of bed and pulled on

Miguel's bathrobe. He was still sleeping soundly and although she wanted to bend over and kiss the vulnerable, full-lipped mouth, she instead tiptoed into the bathroom.

After her shower she went to prepare breakfast. The smell of coffee, bacon, scrambled eggs and toast soon brought Miguel from the bedroom. He stood at the kitchen doorway, sleepily rubbing his smooth, bronzed chest. His dark hair, usually slicked back smoothly, now tumbled over his forehead. He had such an endearing little boy look about him that Marita's heart gave a painful squeeze.

What did she look like first thing in the morning? Living by herself she'd never thought much about that, but now it suddenly filled her with panic. If she were to continue with this affair—for that's what they were obviously having—she would often be waking up in bed with him and having to face him first thing in the morning in bed.

Well, at least this morning, having applied a bit of mascara and lipstick after the shower, she didn't look too bad. Although she'd had to rummage through the bathroom cupboards to find some moisturizer for her face. It was actually meant for hands, but sufficed in a pinch. She might have to start bringing her toiletries with her wherever she went. Just in case. And an extra pair of undies.

"As your second job, I think I'll hire you for my private cook," Miguel said as he seated himself at the table and dug into the breakfast without waiting. "I'm too lazy to cook anything in the morning and always just have dry cereal."

"Cereal's good," Marita said. "But when you visit your mom, doesn't she cook you a good old-fashioned

North American breakfast with bacon and all?"

Miguel laughed. "Oh, God, no." He pushed another forkful of egg into his mouth. "Mother was born in Canada but she's very traditionally Spanish about everything, including food."

Marita poured them both some coffee and sat down at the table across from him. This was something new she was learning about Miguel and it made her hungry for more information. "So what does she give you for breakfast?"

"She makes *cafe con leche*, a very strong coffee with hot milk. And we have some sweet rolls with that."

"Sweet rolls are nice, but cereal's probably better." Marita reached for a slice of his toast. "So how else is she traditional?"

"Hey, that's mine," Miguel cried and tried unsuccessfully to grab the toast back from her. Laughing, she stuffed it in her mouth.

"Oh, she insists we speak Spanish at home," Miguel told her. "And she has lots of knick-knacks and stuff around the house from Spain."

Marita got up to slip more bread into the toaster.

"And she's very traditional about the family name, always talking about how she expects me to have a son to carry on the Cordova name," Miguel went on, blithely unaware that Marita's heart had just taken a huge nose-dive down to her toes.

A son! Well, that was something she certainly wouldn't be able to produce in this lifetime. But, hey, that would never be her job, so no worries. Still, she had trouble coaxing her heart back to its normal location.

"That sounds very traditional. Almost old-fashioned."

"Yeah. She's been harping about the family name ever since I was little, and too young to know what she was talking about."

"Well, what about Angela?" Marita still couldn't help feeling a sense of loss, even though she knew she would never be called upon to produce a Cordova heir. "She could have a baby, couldn't she?"

"Oh, Mother has already given up on her. Angela's thirty-seven, you know, and doesn't even have a steady boyfriend."

"How about adoption?" Marita tried, though she was sure this idea—very weakly vocalized—wouldn't hold water with this traditional madre of his. If Angela failed to produce an heir, Miguel would have to marry a young woman. Which meant their "meaningful relationship" could be very short-lived.

"She could adopt, of course, but that wouldn't satisfy my mother. It wouldn't be 'blood'." He made air quotes around the word, pronouncing it darkly. "That's the important thing to her. Good, red, Spanish, Cordova blood."

Marita's hand, as she handed him a slice of toast, trembled imperceptibly. Those words nailed the coffin shut.

Having emptied his plate, Miguel got up and wiped his mouth on a paper serviette. "We should get started before the day's all gone."

"Started?" Marita drew a blank. She was still reeling from all she'd heard. It meant Miguel was as good as lost to her on any long-term basis. Not that she'd ever really hoped, but . . . Okay, so secretly she'd hoped.

Miguel chuckled. "Modeling. Remember? I'll get showered and dressed and—"

"You're sure I have to do it naked?" Marita asked,

trying to stall for time.

"You promised, young lady. And, hey, at least you don't have to do too much to prep." He headed for the washroom. "You're as good as naked already," he threw over his shoulder.

A few moments later Marita stood in the middle of the atelier, still in Miguel's bathrobe. She had undone the belt but clutched the robe tightly around her. "I feel so weird standing here in the middle of the room," she said, blushing.

Miguel smiled at this unexpected reticence. Considering how abandoned and uninhibited she'd been last night when they had made passionate love, it was somehow endearing now to see her looking so shy and vulnerable.

"Don't you have anywhere more private where I can undress?" Marita asked, frowning. "The spotlights in the ceiling are too bright."

He pointed to a curtained cubicle in one corner of the studio. "You can go in there, if you like. But, personally, I'd love to see you slip off my robe right there in front of me."

Miguel had been looking forward to this session with growing excitement and impatience. The ideas sizzling in his head were crying out for expression and he wanted to start executing them this very minute.

"I appreciate how you might find that somewhat titillating, but—nah." Marita walked to the cubicle and pulled the curtain shut behind her.

"Do I have to come out naked?" she called after a while.

Miguel chuckled. "No, you can put your clothes on."

"Thanks, I'll do that. Throw them over here, please."

"Smart ass. There's a blue sheet you can wrap

around you if you like."

"I like."

Marita emerged, wrapped up to her chin in pale blue satin. "Actually this feels very sexy," she said and rubbed a fistful of fabric against her cheek.

Miguel was busy arranging his art materials, but when he looked up, he stopped and stared at the woman standing before him. As Marita clutched the folds of satin around her, all her beautiful curves were emphasized, reminding him of a Greek statue. He wanted to paint her right then and there. Never mind arranging her in any other pose.

"Darling," he breathed and walked up to her. He felt the slippery satin underneath his hands as he traced the curves of her body, adding to the heady sensation. "I want to start painting you right now, but I also want to make love to you. Such a dilemma," he murmured in her ear. "What should I do first?"

"Please don't make me choose," Marita whispered. "You know what I would say."

"Tell me."

"Start painting!" Marita cried and pulled out of his embrace. "You can get your jollies afterward."

Miguel laughed and yanked the sheet off her. "You're a cruel woman, Marita de Ville."

He positioned her on the raised platform on top of the satin fabric and arranged her limbs the way he wanted. "Now try not to move around too much, my sweet. Or I'll have to dock your pay."

"I get paid for this?" Her eyes glistened with desire and he had to fight the urge to join her on the dais.

"Of course. I pay all my models."

That was a mistake. Marita's face fell and she sat up.

"I forgot. You do this with all your models. All your gorgeous, young models."

"Marita, please—"

But she slid off the platform, her face a picture of dejection.

"And here I imagined I was special. How naïve of me. I don't want to do this any more." She walked toward the cubicle but Miguel caught her and swiftly picked her up in his arms. Damnation. Was he ever going to convince her how he felt about her?

He sat on the platform, holding her on his knees. "You are the most special thing that's ever come into my life," he said. "I've never felt like this about any other woman. Not even close. Do you understand?"

"No."

He gathered up the satin cloth and wrapped it around her shoulders that were stiff with resistance. Gently he stroked her. How could he make her feel secure? How could he get her to trust him?

"Do you think every modeling session is like this?" Miguel asked. "That I want to have my hands all over the models like I do with you?"

Marita nodded. "Uh-huh. With them being so young and desirable." She sounded and looked like a sulky kid.

"Well, it's not that way at all," Miguel said, keeping his voice calm. "This is a business and they're professionals. Some of them model for a living, others do it as a side-line. They're not here for sex, and I always concentrate on my painting."

"That must be hard to do," Marita muttered. "With them being so young and pretty."

The soft stroking was working and Miguel could feel she was starting to come around. "It's not hard at all.

When I paint, I don't think about anything else, as you'll soon see for yourself. If we ever get around to starting."

He continued to caress her and little by little Marita's body relaxed.

Finally she gave a deep sigh. "Okay." Her voice was muffled against his shoulder.

Then, to his relief, she raised her head and asked, "What do you want me to do?"

"I want you to sit on the platform like a good girl, because I do want to start painting before earthly lust replaces my lofty inspirations." He sat her on the dais and got up.

Marita spread out the satin cloth and lay down on it. "Like this?" she asked and struck a goofy pose.

Miguel laughed. "If you persist on being a comic, I won't give you a lunch break."

Three hours later, when Miguel called the session to a halt, Marita stretched her weary limbs and climbed off the dais. "I'm starving."

Miguel now came toward her. He'd thrown aside his paint smock and was unbuttoning his white shirt. "Time for me to get my—what did you offer me earlier? Jollies?"

"Oh, oh." Marita backed off toward the cubicle. "I'm afraid I'm much too tired for any physical exertion. And you should be, too. You've worked very hard, my man." She gave herself a mental high five for not saying "young", although the word had been on the tip of her tongue. Maybe she was learning. At last.

But he didn't look tired.

"I'm ready to work much harder." Miguel kept coming closer, while Marita backed away from him.

He looked downright dangerous, advancing like a bull with his head held low. She gave a nervous laugh as the glint of heat in his eyes made a shiver of excitement run through her.

"Are you sure you're up to it?" Her voice was very thin.

"Up to it? Let me get closer and you can feel how up to it I am," he rumbled darkly. "I'll just grab a condom and—"

Marita started. "You keep condoms in your studio?" For what purpose would he have them here? For sex, of course. Certainly not for blowing into balloons.

Miguel chuckled. "Yes. Now that you're in my life, I've sprinkle condoms everywhere. I always want to be ready."

Marita discarded her doubts and fell into his arms. "Okay, you win," she cried and he covered her mouth with a kiss that made the room spin.

Miguel picked her up and placed her on the platform.

"Let's practise some poses for future sessions," he murmured.

But Marita could hardly hear him above the roar of blood inside her head. And then, because she couldn't wait any longer, she helped him undress, sheathed him, and pulled him down on top of her with an impatient moan.

It was exactly six o'clock and Ron was knocking on the door. Was there no getting rid of him? Marita was expecting Miguel to come after seven to give her a salsa lesson, and instead here was Ron roaming around her building again.

During the three days in Miguel's condo, while

modeling for him, Marita had been able to observe Miguel the artist. It had brought out a totally new side of him. He was so earnest and assiduous, so totally absorbed in his work. She could sense at these times how everything else around him took second place to his art. It could have made her jealous, but she was happy to see him so intensely concentrating on his creation.

Intense and caring. That was the way he was with everything. When dancing, he led in such a way he brought out the best in her, making her look good. When they had sex, he was a passionate lover, always ensuring she was completely satisfied.

Ron let himself in through the door she had left unlocked for Miguel.

"So who was the kind person who let you in today?" Marita asked. "I didn't hear my phone ring."

Ron laughed. "I think some of the residents are starting to recognize me and are letting me in before I have a chance to buzz you."

"Pity."

Ron threw his jacket on the bench in the hall and went into the living room as though he'd been invited. He sat on the couch and patted the cushion beside him. "Come and sit here. I need to talk with you. It's important."

Marita laughed at the ridiculous gesture and seated herself on the armrest of the chair facing him. What on earth was the man after?

"Martha, last time I visited, that young man was here." Ron began. His face was serious and his tone reminded Marita of his elderly uncle George who, while still on this side of eternity, had loved to sprinkle words of wisdom on every family member.

"Yes, he was."

"It looked to me like . . ." Ron paused, as though considering whether to continue or not. He did. "Like you two were having sex."

"Yes, that's correct." Marita deliberately kept her replies short. She knew that irritated Ron, but brought her some measure of wicked satisfaction.

"He's too young." Ron made this sound like an illness that could be cured.

"Oh, believe me, Ron, he's not too young to have sex." Marita shook her head, keeping her face serious. "Not at all."

Ron coughed at this indiscreet bit of information. "You're forty-three." His tone was accusing.

"Thank you for remembering, Ron. And if I'm not wrong, you will soon hit fifty."

"I'm forty-eight," he hastened to corrected her.

"And your wife is—what? Twenty-seven?"

At this, Ron looked slightly embarrassed. "Marita, I feel I have to tell you something. Hillary and I are no longer together. She—er—I decided to leave her."

An obvious lie. "She found someone else, right?"

Ron looked down at his hands, clutched on his lap, and nodded. "Someone younger than you, perhaps?"

Again he nodded.

"And now could you tell me why you are here, Ron, because it's past six o'clock and I want to have my dinner."

Marita knew Ron was flustered, but refused to feel sorry for him. He stretched his neck in the direction of the kitchen from where delicious aromas floated into the living room. "I don't suppose you want to invite me to join you?"

"No," Marita said firmly. "In fact, now that you're

here, I want to tell you for one final time that I do not want you coming around here any more. We are divorced and that is the end of our story."

"It doesn't have to be the end, you know," Ron's voice had an unpleasant whine to it. "We could try one more time. Lots of people give their marriage a second chance."

Marita burst out laughing. "Ron, you are incredible. Get back together with you? I would never, in this life-time, entertain that thought. No way, José! And now, if you'll excuse me—" She rose and walked into the kitchen to stir the pot of bubbling beef stew.

Ron followed her. "You know I still love you, Marita," he said earnestly. His nostrils flared as he sniffed the air.

"Ron, you don't love me. You love my cooking."

All she'd ever wanted out of her marriage was to be loved. Loved for herself and not for her ability to whip up a great meal. Right from the get-go Ron had always praised her cooking. It was probably the reason he'd asked her to marry him. And like a naïve fool, she'd believed his words, thinking he loved her for herself.

"You are wrong. I've always loved your nice narrow waist." His hands gripped her and he drew her against him.

Shuddering with revulsion, Marita pulled herself free. "Do. Not. Touch. Me. Ron Osmar." The words, pronounced with a ferocity that was so unlike her, made him back away.

His eyes narrowed with anger. "You're making a fool of yourself with that young man, you know," he growled.

Marita's sarcastic laughter made him take another step back. "Of course you have first-hand experience in those matters, Ron. But I definitely don't want, or need, any advice from you. You look after your own marital mess." She looked him straight in the eye and this time she didn't even try to be kind. "I want you to leave, Ron, and I do not want you to come knocking on my door ever again. Do you understand?" She went into the hall and picked up his jacket from the bench. "If you come here again I'll call the police and they will put a restraining order on you."

Ron's face grew red and twisted into an ugly grimace. "All our friends are talking about you. Everyone says you're a cougar."

There was that word again. Marita strove to keep her voice even. "And I suppose you're the one who has kindly supplied your friends with all the details of my private life?"

"He'll leave you, too!" Ron shouted. "They all do. He'll find someone younger. And prettier. Don't say I didn't warn you."

"That's my concern," Marita ground out between her teeth. If he wasn't gone in three seconds she would explode.

"You're too old for him," he spat out. "Cougar!"

Without a word Marita opened the door and gave him a helpful push out into the hall. She threw his jacket after him and slammed the door shut as hard as she could. She hoped that sound would ring in his ears forever. Violent tremors of anger shook through her as she stood facing the closed door.

She returned to the kitchen, sat down at the table, and let her head drop into her arms. Damn! Ron was right of course. Some day she would be sorry, because from what Miguel had told her about his mother, eventually he would leave her for someone younger.

Yes, he'd called her the most special thing in his life, and had said he'd never felt this way about any other woman. And maybe he thought she was special now, but one day he would wake up and realize he needed someone who could give him a child. A grandson for his mother.

Marita sat up and squared her shoulders. But she was not going to be the one to end it. No way, José! She would enjoy this ride right to the end. Life might only give her this one chance to experience something this wonderful, and she was going to hold onto it for all it was worth, as long as she could.

But a cougar?

Damn it all! That sounded so vulgar.

Chapter Nine

Steve wasn't giving up. And Marita had to confess that after Ron's ugly words and Rosalyn's put-downs, hearing Steve's kind voice on the phone were like healing ointment on a wound.

"I've been thinking a lot about you," Steve said when he called again one evening. "I know you don't want to be my girlfriend because of Miguel, but as I said before, I hope you're still my friend."

"Of course I'm your friend, Steve," Marita said. "Why not?" What was the man getting at?

"Well, I'm having a small get-together with a few friends to celebrate the fact I've survived for half a century on this earth, and I would like for you to come."

"Fifty years? Steve, you certainly don't look it." And it was a fact, because he didn't. Maybe forty-five. "I assume the 'you' includes Miguel?"

"Of course," Steve said too quickly, making it obvious he'd made the invitation only to her. "You and Miguel."

"We'd love to come." At least she hoped Miguel would love to come. "I'll ask him."

As soon as Steve had given her the details, Marita rang up Miguel, but was disappointed when he sounded less than enthusiastic about the idea.

"You know damn well he doesn't want me to come. Only you," Miguel grumbled and Marita had to cede him that point. "But he's in luck, because I can't make it that night anyway. I'm helping Anita get ready for her art show on Sunday."

"Oh? You didn't tell me about that." Or mention Anita. Come to think of it, he hadn't told her very much about his friends. In fact, she knew practically zilch about his life outside the salsa club and the art classes. Except now she knew he had a pretty sister and a traditional Spanish mother who yearned for a grandchild.

"Didn't I? I guess I forgot," Miguel said, much too matter-of-factly.

She wished he'd remembered. Unless he didn't think it was important that she knew. "Well, that's too bad. I'll bring you some birthday cake."

"You mean you're still going?" Miguel sounded incredulous. "I thought since I couldn't make it—"

"Of course I'll go. He's my friend. Why wouldn't I go?"

"Because he's a friend who would like to have you as a girlfriend. That's why. To me that puts a different spin on things."

This talk of boyfriends and girlfriends sounded so juvenile. "I hope you and I are way past that kind of melodrama, Miguel," she said. "You know you're my one and only, and Steve knows it too, but surely we can still have other friends in our lives."

That was another thing they had never discussed.

Miguel was silent for a moment. "You're right. We

each have our own lives, our own work, friends, family and our own interests. They're outside our relationship." His voice sounded too dismissive, somehow too casual.

Now it was Marita's turn to be silent. Did she want to be that independent of him? No. That's not what she wanted at all. She wanted to share his life and his work, at least for now. Maybe he didn't feel the same way, because why should he bother to get too up-close and personal with some temporary girlfriend? Meaningful, yes, but not permanent.

"Is that what you want?" she asked in a small voice. She closed her eyes and crossed her fingers. Please let him say no.

"No!" The word thundered out so strong and decisive that the sun burst through into Marita's heart. "That's not what I want. But I'd rather talk about this face to face," he added. "Not on the phone."

"When I come over for the next modeling session?"

"Yes."

"But Steve's party is tomorrow evening. You're sure you can't make it?"

"I'm sure," Miguel replied. "But you go ahead and have fun." Then he added with a smile in his voice, "But not too much fun."

Marita came home from Steve's party alone in a cab, after declining his offer to accompany her home. Wine had flowed easily, along with the conversation and laughter, and Marita had to admit she'd enjoyed being with Steve's friends. Could it have been because they were all from her own age group? In fact, she'd probably been one of the youngest there. Yes, that had felt damned good. Almost like being a kid again.

The word "old" hadn't even popped out of her mouth, except when she'd teased Steve about him having reached the half-century mark. But she hadn't once directed the word at herself. For which she now gave herself a pat on the back.

Steve had been very attentive all evening, always making sure she didn't lack for anything—food, wine or company. He was actually a fun guy, in a helpless kind of way, and his friends all seemed to be very fond of him. When they asked about her part in his life— and as his close friends they probably felt they had the right to know—Steve had explained she was a new friend from the Spadina Salsa Club. But he'd said it in such a way, with his arm around her shoulders, that it gave the impression there was more to their relationship than he was telling. His friends nodded, smiling. They understood—or thought they did. And Marita hadn't felt like denying anything, because that's exactly what she was—a new friend from the Spadina Salsa Club. After that the people easily included her in their conversation, as someone who was special to their good friend, Steve.

Yes, it had been a fun evening.

As soon as Marita got home, she checked her messages. There was one from Miguel about the art show. They had completed the set-up and he asked her to come to a private viewing of the work at the Four Winds Gallery before the show opened to the public the following week. They could go on Sunday afternoon, right after the modeling session if that was all right with her.

Of course it was. Meeting his friends was exactly what she wanted to do. And, come to think of it, by modeling for him, wasn't she already sharing in his work and his life, just as she wanted?

In Miguel's atelier Marita undressed and stood naked in front of him, now feeling totally at ease.

"How's this?" she asked and struck a racy pose. "Lovely?"

Miguel laughed and threw a dry sponge at her. "Get up on the platform, woman, and stop clowning," he said. "This is serious business."

Marita giggled as she climbed onto the dais. It felt so wonderfully freeing to know Miguel adored her body and loved to see her nude. And when they made love he always wanted the lights on.

How different from being married to Ron. She'd felt his critical eye on her whenever he glimpsed a part of her nude body. Especially her backside. And he'd let her know all about her flaws in no uncertain terms. She'd always kept herself covered and made sure she was well under the bed sheets before he joined her in bed. And if he sometimes had wanted sex, it had happened with the lights out, of course.

"I want to get my fill of your perfect body," Miguel always told her as he caressed her curves. He made her feel desirable and she trusted him not to hurt her. Even though she knew the day of reckoning was in the offing. But she pushed that thought deep down, out of the way of her happiness.

"I'm afraid we don't have time for lovemaking today," Miguel said ruefully after the session was over. "But we'll make up for it next week."

She wet her lips sensuously as she started to put on her bra and panties, making her moves as alluring as possible. "Umm, I can hardly wait."

Miguel laughed. "If you don't stop those seductive

moves right now, we won't get to the gallery at all."

He stripped out of his work pants and stood there in his shorts, his arousal in plain view. "But since I'm almost undressed anyway, how about a quickie?" He approached her, his arms outstretched.

But Marita quickly grabbed her silk print dress from a nearby chair and slipped it over her head. "Sorry, I'm all dressed for the party. Just have to slip my shoes on."

Grumbling, Miguel went to get his clothes and pulled on his navy pants and blue dress shirt. He left his deep red tie hanging loosely around his neck.

Marita reached up to tighten it, but he stopped her. "I wear it loose, like this," he said. "It's part of 'the look'." He put air quotes around the word and added, with his to-die-for grin, "Doesn't it look good on me?"

Of course anything looked good on him. And Marita was sure he knew it, too. "Yes, darling, you're one helluva charmer," she said and gave him a smacking kiss on the lips. "Now let's get going."

She remembered the Four Winds Gallery from last spring, when Shaylee had her successful art exhibit and sale there. Max, the proprietor, once again was there as the beaming host and talked up Anita's paintings, making it obvious he was looking forward to good sales when the exhibit opened up to the public.

Carrying her wine glass, Marita wandered among the guests. Miguel was chatting with his friends and co-artists and had left her to fend for herself. That didn't bother her, but something else did. It took a while before she could put a finger on this feeling of unease.

The invited crowd was very young.

Yikes! With a sinking feeling, Marita saw she was

probably the oldest person in the room, with the probable exception of Max. Did they all know she was with Miguel? And—the thought made her almost sick to her stomach—did they consider her a cougar?

Cougar! Her cheeks began to burn and she looked desperately around for something to distract her before she sank through the floor from embarrassment. She made a dash for the hors d'oeuvre table where she could turn her back on the people while she quickly piled up her plate.

God! Now everyone would think she was starving. She considered putting some of the stuff back but that would have been as rude as double-dipping.

"Hi there," a voice beside her forced Marita to turn around. The woman was probably not much older than Lisa.

"We haven't been introduced, but my name is Ella. I saw you come in with Miguel. You must be his new girlfriend."

"Well, I don't know if I'd go that far," Marita said and, without thinking, she stuffed a cracker with pâté into her mouth. "I certainly wouldn't classif—" her words were muffled by the food.

"Pardon me?" Ella asked.

Marita waved a hand in front of her mouth to indicate she couldn't speak. After swallowing the dry cracker with great difficulty, she continued, feeling like a total rube. "I was saying I'm not actually Miguel's girlfriend. Not in so many words. I'd probably rather say a very good friend."

What the hell was she saying? Not in so many words? She'd been having steamy sex with Miguel for weeks but "in so many words" she wasn't his girlfriend?

"I've heard you two are a hot number," the young woman interrupted. "Are you saying you're friends with benefits?" She smiled.

Marita couldn't tell if the woman's smile was friendly or sarcastic. She couldn't trust herself to tell the difference. She was probably reading unfriendly meanings into perfectly innocent comments. That's what happened when you suspected that everyone considered you a cougar.

Friends with benefits? Was that all they were? Something new for her to chew on. To chew on. She popped a tiny meat pie into her mouth. Damn! She hadn't meant to do that in the middle of the conversation. She dabbed her mouth.

But before she could reply to Ella's question, Miguel turned up behind her. "Marita, I've been wanting to introduce you to a few more of my friends," he said. "So let's start with Ella, here. Ella, this is my girlfriend, Marita."

Oops! Marita cringed. Now what?

"Your girlfriend?" Ella raised her beautifully plucked eyebrows, and Marita was absolutely sure this surprise was not genuine. "But Marita just told me she's not your girlfriend. She indicated you're just friends with benefits. What is going on here?"

Miguel frowned at Marita. "Yes, what indeed?"

He took her by the elbow, leaving Ella to stand with an amused smile on her face.

"Is there something I should know?" he demanded, when they reached a quiet corner.

"I was just—" How was she going to explain this? "We've never—" she tried again. And then she decided to bite the bullet. "You know very well you've never introduced me as your girlfriend to anyone," she burst out defensively. "So how'm I supposed to know what you've told your friends about me? Wouldn't I sound pretty foolish if I told everyone I'm your girlfriend and you had told them we're only friends? Eh?"

Miguel frowned. "But I've told you I love you. Surely that should tell you I consider you mine."

"No you haven't," Marita countered.

Miguel's frown deepened. Obviously he was totally confused. "I haven't what?"

People were beginning to throw curious glances at them but there was nowhere they could go for a private conversation. Stepping outside was not an option, not with the chilly autumn wind whipping the last fallen leaves along the wet sidewalks.

"You haven't ever told me you love me," Marita insisted in a loud whisper. "You said I was special, and you'd never felt like this about any other woman. But I don't recall you saying you love me or asking me to be your girl."

Marita knew she was splitting hairs. Here they'd been having mad sex for weeks and she was saying ridiculous things about being asked to be his girlfriend. No wonder the poor man was confused.

"This isn't like you, Marita," Miguel said. His voice held an edge of irritation. "I thought I'd made my feelings perfectly clear. I never knew I had to ask you. I just assumed—"

"Well, you shouldn't assume." Yes, she sounded childishly sullen and defiant, but she had to hold her ground. She was feeling far from secure about her place in his life because they'd never discussed it. "If you don't tell me, how am I supposed to know?"

Miguel threw up his hands. "I don't understand you and I'm not going to talk about it here, with fifty pairs of ears listening in." His mouth tight with anger, he turned and marched off to talk to Mika, who was inspecting a nearby painting very closely. And probably had heard every word.

Standing there, alone and bereft, Marita didn't dare to look around her for fear of seeing pity or, worse still, amusement, on all the faces. She pushed another hors d'oeuvre into her mouth and almost gagged.

Then she saw Mika turn to look at her. Obviously Miguel was expressing his frustration to him. She shrugged. Well, let him. Defiantly she turned her back on the men and forced herself to make a brave attempt at mingling with the guests. Although she smiled and chatted with a few of them, she couldn't remember a time when she'd felt this completely out of her element.

A group of young women was standing by the bar. Was she being paranoid, or were some of them glancing at her surreptitiously? She strolled toward them, but when she got close, she could have sworn the conversation was cut short. A couple of them turned to face her.

"Marita, it's so nice you were able to come, dear," one of the girls said, smiling kindly.

Dear? The word made Marita feel about seventy years old. Luckily the girl hadn't said "dearie" or she would have started to look for her cane.

"It's so nice to be here, my dear," Marita responded. A little devil in her made her voice sound old and feeble.

Surprise and shock registered on the girl's face, but with an innocent smile, Marita turned and walked to the bar to ask for vodka on the rocks.

Carrying the drink, she wandered around, observing how the young men and women were dressed. Like the strutting models on the fashion pages of the daily newspaper, that's how! She'd always assumed normal people really didn't wear those kinds of clothes, but it was obvious they really did. And it left her feeling dowdy in her simple silk print dress that reached down to her knees. The high heels she always wore because of her short stature were about the only thing she had in common with these youngsters. But even they suddenly looked to her like a twenty-year-old pair from a used-clothing store.

At Steve's party most of the men wore suits, which had looked perfectly fine. These young men—she could have called them boys—were dressed in such a variety of get-ups that Miguel's dark blue shirt and loose red tie looked almost normal. All these young people were chatting, laughing and drinking, very much like the guests at Steve's party had been. But this talk was about subjects Marita didn't connect with. In fact there was something about the whole atmosphere, including the loud music, that made her want to gracefully back out the door and disappear into the windy night.

She did not belong here.

Without Miguel by her side, she felt lonely and forgotten, like the Velveteen Rabbit in the picture book she'd purchased while pregnant with her baby. Her eyes filled and she was sorry she'd started the argument with Miguel. It was so stupid of her to question his feelings toward her, because she was sure he truly believed what he told her. She was very special to him—at this moment. But that didn't mean one day he wouldn't meet someone young and beautiful and feel that woman was even more special. At which point Marita would do a graceful exit left. Or right. Or maybe straight down into the orchestra pit.

She snorted at the melodramatic thought. But she also knew she would be one badly hurting woman.

Marita was relieved when Miguel finally came and told her they were leaving. She'd felt like such an idiot, wandering around by herself, nervously picking at the hors d'oeuvres from the plate she continued to carry around for a crutch. Only a few people had stopped to chat politely with her for a minute or two.

On the way home in the darkness of Miguel's car she decided to make her declaration.

"I think we've been too hasty."

"With regards to—?"

"Our relationship," Marita said and swallowed hard.

Miguel brought the car to a screeching stop against the curb, turned the motor off and turned to face her. "What are you talking about Marita?"

"Look, Miguel, I've thought long and hard about this relationship of ours. It isn't going to work, and I'm pulling out." She fought to speak without emotion, to keep from revealing the turmoil raging inside her.

"Oh, are you now? Just like that?" His voice was unpleasant and sarcastic.

"No, not just like that. I said I've thought about it all evening. I mean for a long time."

"And could you tell me what, exactly, made you come to this conclusion?"

His tone annoyed her and she slapped her knee. "Stop talking like that, Miguel. I'm not enjoying this, you know."

"Neither am I," he said evenly. "Now please explain what this is all about. Has it anything to do with our earlier discussion about your position in my life?"

"Yes, partly," she admitted. "But the reality is, tonight I finally faced what I've been trying very hard to ignore."

"Which is—?"

"I'm too old for you, Miguel."

"No, you are not," Miguel exploded. "You are exactly right for me. In every possible way."

He reached over to take her hand but Marita quickly pulled it away. She knew his touch would make her resolve crumble like a dyke in a tsunami.

"I'm sorry I got annoyed with you," Miguel said, his voice contrite. "But it sounded so stupid when you said you didn't know you were my girlfriend. Because you're much more than that to me. You're my love."

Marita almost burst into tears at the sincerity flowing through his words. Yes, she knew he meant every word now when they were passionate lovers. But how would he feel in a few months? A few years?

"Miguel, it's not about your feelings for me," Marita said, trying to keep her eyes from filling and spoiling her determination. "I know you mean every word. But it's no use kidding ourselves. I am too old for you. Tonight I felt downright ancient when I was with your friends. They're too young. Don't you get it?"

"No, I don't get it," he declared. "Most of them are no younger than I am."

"I rest my case." She folded her hands on her lap.

"Marita, stop this!"

She could tell he was getting annoyed, but pressed on. "When I was at Steve's birthday party last night, I had such a great time. I felt comfortable with him and with his friends. The music was appropriate. We chatted and laughed and I didn't feel out of sync with anyone or anything. I didn't feel old. In fact I actually felt young."

Miguel was silent, but Marita could almost feel his

fury sizzling through the darkness. Still, she had to continue.

"Tonight at the gallery I didn't know what to say, how to communicate with those . . . those children. I even felt dowdy in my nice party dress. They were all dressed like models from the latest fashion magazine and made me look like some freak from fifty years ago."

"You looked lovely. You were the prettiest girl there."

"Too little, too late, Miguel. Too bad you didn't say that when I put the dress on. That would have given me something to fall back on at the party. I'm not saying I didn't look nice. It's just that I looked so different from all the young women there."

Miguel sighed and threw up his hands in a gesture of despair. "Who cares about clothes? That's nothing to do with us."

"Miguel, it's the same dress I had on at Steve's party. He told me I looked beautiful, and what's more important, I felt beautiful. Young and beautiful. Not like a cougar."

She knew she'd hit the nerve when, without a word, Miguel turned away from her, started the car and drove on. She had wounded this young, Spanish man's pride, talking about how another man had made her feel. She almost wished she hadn't said it. She'd made it sound like Miguel never made her feel beautiful. Which was so wrong! Didn't he always tell her how perfect she was? Didn't he caress her and let her know he adored her?

But the words had done the trick. If she'd wanted to end the relationship, she couldn't have done it any better, because it was now over. Miguel would never want anything to do with her again. And rightly so.

The drive to her apartment building was much

faster than the speed limit allowed, and Marita was relieved the hour was late and no police cruisers were patrolling that section of Yonge Street.

Miguel accompanied her up to her apartment. He waited until she had dug out her key and had unlocked the door.

"Good-bye," he said and turned to go down the stairwell. He didn't look back.

"Good-bye, Miguel," she whispered to his back.

He was gone.

At work Marita was thankful a couple of big new assignments were taking up her time. She submerged herself into recipe books and brochures, and tried to ignore her aching heart. That, of course, was impossible, but everyone commented how funny her jokes were these days.

At home, however, it was difficult to hide her sadness from Lisa.

"What's wrong, Marita," the girl asked for the umpteenth time. "Are you positive you're not sick?"

"I'm positive," Marita replied. "I think it's the autumn blues." She flipped through the TV channel, looking for a movie that would make her laugh.

"I've never heard of the autumn blues," Lisa said with narrowed eyes. "I've heard of the seasonal affective disorder but it doesn't hit people till winter."

"I probably just got it earlier than most," Marita said. "Do you want to watch this Danny Kaye flick?"

"No thanks. I don't care for Danny Kaye. Have you had S.A.D. before?" Lisa asked, eyeing Marita suspiciously.

"Oh, I'm sure I have," Marita replied casually. "I may be a funny lady but I do get the blues when winter comes. Long dark nights and all that. Why don't you like Danny Kaye?" She flipped the TV off and placed the converter on the coffee table.

"He tries so hard to be funny it backfires." Lisa got up from the couch and headed for her room. "I have reading to do." She stopped and turned around. "How come Miguel hasn't been here for salsa lessons?"

"Oh, we decided to stop them. Didn't I tell you?" She didn't dare to look up and bare her soul to Lisa's perceptive eyes.

"No, you didn't tell me. Why did you stop?" Lisa demanded.

Such a persistent pest she was.

"Because I'm so good," Marita said. "I outshine everyone at the Spadina Club and Miguel is getting jealous of my dancing skills."

Lisa didn't join in the banter. "I think something's happened," she said with a serious face.

Marita threw a sofa cushion at her. "Go do your homework, young lady, and stop grilling me. You're beginning to sound like your mother."

Shaking her head, Lisa withdrew into her bedroom. "Something's happened, I know it has," she muttered.

Steve called to say hello. Miguel, however, didn't. Just the way it was supposed to be, Marita told herself. But the starving need inside her still kept her hoping he would call and ease the hunger.

Surely this ache would eventually go away. She'd lived long enough to know everything got better with time. She wasn't a teenager, filled with despair, who believed the pain in her heart would be there for the rest of her life. She was a middle-aged, sensible adult, and she knew it would take a long time before this hurt would dissolve. But in time it would.

So she tried to immerse herself in her work. She flipped through volumes of cook books and wrote reams of plans on how to feed hundreds of people at dozens of parties. It didn't seem to help.

It would just take time.

She watched old comedies on TV, but had to agree with Lisa that Danny Kaye tried too hard to be funny. And Jerry Lewis was too ridiculous. And even an old Peter Sellers movie couldn't make her laugh.

It would take more time.

When Steve called one beautiful autumn day to invite her for a drive, she agreed. After all, why should she avoid all men just because Miguel didn't call? And since it was obvious Miguel never would call, should she sit at home and mope for the rest of her natural born days? No way, José!

The day turned out to be very enjoyable, except Marita wished it was Miguel sitting beside her. Steve was pleasant company, but he couldn't make her laugh the way Miguel did with his boyish antics. And as they drove along the country roads, she could imagine Miguel's animated eagerness over the exquisite fall colours, which were more glorious than they'd been in years.

"A great year for colours," Steve commented.

"Sure is."

"Should have brought my camera."

"Right. Me too."

They stopped for coffee at a bakery-cafe in a quaint village with the romantic name of Violet Hill. But somehow Marita didn't feel romantic as she munched on a dry tea biscuit. To be fair, she'd ordered it herself, but Miguel would have ordered sticky buns for them both, and together they would have laughed and licked their fingers.

Marita pictured the two of them enjoying the treat, and she smiled. Steve smiled back at her. "It's a lovely day," he said.

"Yes, it is," she replied. "Thank you for asking me out." And she meant it. Anything was better than sitting by herself at home.

"What's Miguel doing today?" Steve wanted to know. "Is he busy with an art project?"

Should she tell him? Well, it was no use pretending Miguel was coming back, so Steve might as well know the score. She swallowed a piece of tea biscuit before replying. "Actually, Miguel and I have decided to call it quits."

At the news Steve face broke into a wide grin of pleasure. "You have? That's great." Then he realized his faux pas and his expression sobered. "I'm sorry, I didn't mean it the way it came out. I only meant—"

Marita patted his arm. "I know what you meant, Steve. It's okay."

"So, then, is it too early to ask you to come to the Danforth Salsa Club with me next Wednesday?"

Marita could tell he was trying to hide his eagerness. She hesitated. Dancing salsa was the last thing she felt like doing at the moment. Especially without Miguel. But she knew activity was a cure for everything, and sitting around at home was definitely not helpful.

"Sure, Steve," she said at last. "I think that would be fun."

Like hell it would. But probably more fun than having a root canal.

Chapter Ten

The days passed and Miguel didn't call. Of course Marita didn't expect him to, but couldn't stop herself from hoping, no matter how insane that was.

Steve phoned often during the week, which helped to distract her and prevented her from watching old romantic re-runs, feeling sorry for herself and shedding useless tears.

Once Lisa caught her simply staring at the screen.

"What are you watching?" Lisa asked.

Marita started. "I have no idea," she confessed and blinked in confusion.

Shaking her head Lisa went to her room.

On Wednesday evening Steve dutifully came to pick her up for the Danforth Salsa Club. Marita couldn't have been less enthusiastic about going, and she had to do the best acting of her life so he wouldn't see her reluctance. He was so attentive and kind it would have been cruel to tell him she'd almost been sick to her stomach getting ready.

The atmosphere at the Danforth Club was similar to the Spadina. The dim lighting, the tables and chairs by the wall and the swirling beams of coloured light almost made her expect to see Miguel dancing among the swaying bodies on the floor.

"Let's boogie," Steve said as soon as he had procured them a table.

At first Marita had to will her hips to undulate and force her feet to move, but to her surprise she was soon drawn into the beat of the salsa rhythm. Before long she found herself actually enjoying the dancing. And yet, whenever Steve held her close, she couldn't help wishing it had been Miguel's hard body pressing against her.

At the end of the evening Steve drove her home and accompanied her to her door. He stood there, obviously expecting to come in.

"It's late and Lisa is sleeping," Marita said.

"Tomorrow is Sunday," Steve said. "Even if her sleep is disturbed a bit, she can sleep in."

Damn! He was right, of course. In fact, Marita wasn't absolutely sure if Lisa was in or out at the moment. Wouldn't it look great if she were to come traipsing down the hall at this very moment, returning from a—

Lisa stepped out of the elevator. "Hi, Marita. Hi, Steve," she said in a cheery whisper. "Looks like we all got here the same time."

Marita fumbled with her key to hide her embarrassed face. "Oh, goodness, I thought you'd be in by now, Lisa." She opened the door and let them all in.

Lisa removed her coat and boots. "Pete and I got talking and didn't see the time fly by," she said and added dreamily, "He's so-o nice."

"I haven't met this Pete," Marita said. "Are you sure he's a boy your mother would approve of?" She hung up her coat but didn't offer to take Steve's. Maybe he would take the hint and leave.

"Yes, he is. But what's more important, he's a boy I approve of," Lisa said. "I'm an independent woman. Like you."

"Oh, are you now?" Marita said dryly. "So I guess your mother doesn't have to give you a living allowance any more?"

Lisa laughed. "My independence doesn't go quite that far." She gave Marita's cheek a quick peck. "Good night, Steve. I'm off to bed," she said and disappeared into her room.

Steve still stood there, looking a bit lost.

Marita couldn't help feeling sorry for him. "Would you like a cup of coffee before you drive off, Steve?"

He brightened visibly. "Yes, I would, thanks." He removed his down jacket and flung it on the hall bench while Marita went into the kitchen to fill the coffee pot.

He sat at the kitchen table to watch her. "I had a very nice time tonight. I hope you did, too."

Marita was happy to be fussing with the coffee filter so she didn't have to face him. "Yes, I did," she said and hoped she sounded convincing. "I enjoyed the exercise." Because that's all she had enjoyed. It had felt so wrong whenever Steve had held her close and moved his body against hers. Even though they had done it so many times before, something was different. Maybe because Miguel had always been there, ready to claim her after the dance and to show Steve she belonged to him. She didn't want Steve to get the idea he could usurp Miguel's place in her heart even if Miguel was no longer in the picture.

"I was thinking maybe tomorrow we could drive along the lake shore and—" Steve began, but Marita interrupted him.

"I'm sorry, Steve, but I have a load of work to catch up on." And she did. Of course it was something she could have done in the evening, if she'd really wanted to go with him.

"That's too bad. Well, maybe next week we could go dancing again. You wouldn't want all of Miguel's hard work to go to waste, would you?"

What an unfortunate thing for him to say. Marita bit her lip and continued to fuss needlessly with the coffee preparations. "Can't get these darned filters to separate," she muttered.

But eventually the coffee was ready, and had been drunk, and Steve was finally on his way home.

Marita collapsed into her bed, and gave way to her tears.

"You know, Marita, you seem to have lost a bit of your former sparkle," Steve remarked as they sat at a table at the Spadina. Marita hadn't wanted to come here, but didn't want to tell Steve she was afraid of running into Miguel. Maybe even Miguel plus Jessica.

"I think I've just been working too hard the past week," Marita assured him. "Nothing that a good rest won't cure." Or being in Miguel's arms. That would have been the best medicine of all.

But that medicine was all sold out at the pharmacy.

"We'll dance slowly tonight," Steve said. "And go home early. Okay?"

"That would be good, Steve." He was such a caring guy. "Thanks for understanding. But I want you to go and boogie while I take it easy."

"As long as you don't mind."

While Steve was off doing some fast dancing, Marita

sat at the table and looked around the room. She thought back to the first time she'd come here and how the sensuous moves had seemed almost indecent. Now she could see that the dancers were simply having a good time, letting the rhythm free their bodies to move with abandon. Of course most of them followed the basic steps, but there were many who seemed to be moving just for the love of moving, like she'd done when she first started out.

All at once an electric shock went through her and she felt his presence even before she heard him.

"Marita." The deep voice behind her made her swing around.

A choked cry escaped from her lips. "Miguel!" She wanted to stand up, but her legs had gone limp.

"Dance with me?" his quiet voice entreated her. He held out his hands and she grasped them tightly. With a groan he pulled her up and pressed her tightly against him.

"Marita." He buried his face against her neck and held her. Held her. He didn't ever want to let her go. The pain that had filled him for almost three weeks, now poured out of him replaced by an incredible sense of peace. Happiness flowed through him, as though he'd inhaled some soothing drug.

"I love you, Marita" he whispered fiercely. "I love you." And then, at last, he kissed the lips he'd missed so achingly, rinsing away the last vestige of anguish inside him. It was as though magically all the broken pieces of him had come together, making him whole again.

"Nothing matters to me but you," he muttered against her hair. "I don't care about anything else but having you with me. We'll only go to Steve's parties if you want. Hell, we'll make sixty-year-old friends so you'll always feel like a little kid when we're with them, if that's what you want. Darling, I just want you to be happy."

Marita's laughter bubbled out, exactly the way he loved to hear it. And when she looked at him her eyes sparkled with love. With love for him! It was so palpable he could almost touch it. "I want you to be happy," he repeated. "And I want you to marry me. Please, darling?"

She leaned her head against his chest. "Hold me, Miguel," she whispered.

And he did, all dancing forgotten. The woman he loved was securely in his arms again. "Will you, Marita? Will you marry me?"

From the way her face shone, he could tell what her answer would be even before she spoke.

"I will," she whispered. "With all my heart. Miguel, you'll never know how much I've missed you. How much I love you."

Steve came back to the table, slightly out of breath and Miguel saw the surprise on his face.

Marita smiled at him from inside Miguel's embrace. "Steve, we have—" she began, but Steve interrupted her with a laugh.

"Hey, you don't have to say a word. You haven't looked this happy for weeks. All I ask is an invitation to your wedding."

He held out his hand to Miguel. "Congratulations, young man. You know you've got yourself one fabulous woman. Lucky you."

Miguel grinned. "Yeah, I know." He couldn't even feel any animosity toward the man who'd been encroaching on his territory. "I hope you don't mind if

I take her away with me now."

"It wouldn't matter if I minded or not, because I know she'd never come with me. So go ahead and steal her away, with my blessing."

As soon as they reached Miguel's condo and had removed their coats, he picked her up in his arms. Incredible relief filled him now that she was here again and he carried her into his bedroom and laid her down on his bed like a most precious gift.

"I wish I had a ring to give you right now to make it official, my darling fiancée," he said as he began to undress her.

He loved to do this—slowly uncover each and every beautiful part of her for him to admire and devour. She was so damned beautiful. And she was all his. He still found it difficult to believe his wonderful luck.

"That's okay," Marita said. She stretched herself tantalizingly and grinned. "I'll let you make love to me even without a ring. I'm that kind of a woman."

Miguel removed her bra. "Just the kind I love," he growled, taking one nipple into his mouth. "But I have to say you've given me a damned difficult time the last few weeks. They've been the worst in my entire life. Don't do it to me ever again, my darling."

"Likewise, my love," Marita whispered, all joking gone out of her voice. "I never want to go through that awful anguish again."

"We never will," Miguel assured her. And with a deep sigh of satisfaction he slid his hands along her softly rounded curves, now totally exposed to him. Something he'd only dreamed about with an aching yearning.

Her soft lips welcomed him. After exploring her mouth he began to kiss her body, caressing every beloved part, until she moaned with longing. He entered her with deliberate slowness, holding her eyes with his throughout the lovemaking, so she would know the depth of his love for her. Hungrily he took in every nuance of her growing passion, until the blinding climax exploded in him, blacking out the world.

Afterward, Marita fingered his earlobe. "You know what we're going to do tomorrow?"

"More of the same, I hope," Miguel replied. "I don't think I'll let you out of my bed till Monday morning." Lazily he stretched, one limb at a time. "We'll just lie here and order in food. And you can be my appetizer and my dessert."

Marita laughed. "Hey, I like your idea better than mine, but I think mine is more practical."

"Which is. . . ?"

"We'll drive to Kingston to visit my parents. I want them to meet you in person."

"That sounds like a plan," Miguel said. "And maybe the following weekend we can drive to Kleinburg to make the big announcement to my mother."

His mother! Marita froze and suddenly all the joy poured out of her. What had she been thinking, agreeing to marry Miguel? In the blinding ecstasy of seeing him again and being in his arms, she had totally forgotten about his mother and her expectations.

"What's the matter?" Miguel asked, frowning. "Why this sudden serious face?"

"Oh, nothing. I suddenly remembered that my parents may not be home tomorrow."

What poppycock. She'd been talking with her mother on the phone a couple of days ago and knew very well they were going to be spending the day watching a football game. One of her father's favourite sports on TV.

"That's no problem. Give them a call and if they're not home, we can just revert to my plan." Miguel reached for her but she slipped out of his arms.

Marriage was impossible. It could never happen. Oh God, why had she said yes to him? But right now she didn't want to talk about it, because it would cause a quarrel and an absolutely final breakup which she simply could not deal with. Not after just getting him back again. She knew she would die if she had to spend the rest of her life without him.

If? The word, of course, was "when".

They would go to see her parents tomorrow and somehow she would fudge her way out of announcing their engagement. Because there was not going to be any engagement.

And as for her and Miguel—they would carry on as before, as lovers, until she was forced to make the final announcement and tell him it was over.

Tall, mature maples, now leafless and bare, lined the street where the Gordon house sat in a neat, straight row of very similar yellow brick bungalows.

Marita hurried up the walk with excited steps. Her parents were precious to her and she always loved to return home. She opened the front door and yodeled, "Mom, Dad, we're here!"

Mrs. Gordon came out to meet them, wiping her hands on a towel. "Welcome home, dear," she caroled and gave Marita a hug and a kiss on the cheek. "How are you, Miguel?" she said and extended her hand to him with a warm smile.

Marita was happy to see Miguel pull her mother into

a warm hug. "I'm so happy to meet you at last," he said. "Marita has told me so many wonderful things about you."

"Oh, balderdash!" With a self-depreciating wave Mrs. Gordon dismissed his words, laughing at his supposed joke.

The house was modest but spacious, and in the living room Mr. Gordon was waiting in his wheelchair to welcome them, his long legs wrapped in a shawl. Marita had told Miguel about her father's debilitating stroke ten years earlier, when he'd been seventy-five.

She bent down to give him a kiss on the forehead.

"Hello, dear," he said and then turned to Miguel. "I'm glad Martha brought a fine young man with her. It's nice to have some male company once in a while to take my side on issues."

"My dad keeps calling me Martha," Marita whispered to Miguel when they were out of earshot. "He can't seem to get used to my new name and I don't want to nag him about it."

"Martha's a fine, old name," Miguel whispered back.

Yes, that was the problem. It was old. Like she was. Marita wanted to kick herself for thinking like this but couldn't help it.

When lunch was ready, Marita and Miguel helped set the dining room table.

"I brought some champagne for a surprise celebration," Miguel told her. "I have it in a cooler in the car. Could you put out some glasses?"

Marita winced. It surprised her, all right. "You shouldn't have, Miguel," she said, trying not to be annoyed with him for spoiling her plan.

"Why not? Are your parents teetotalers? You didn't tell me."

"Well, champagne doesn't usually go with vegetable soup and grilled cheese sandwiches," Marita said, but she knew her explanation was lame.

"Champagne goes with anything when it's celebration time," he said, but looked puzzled at her reaction. "What's the matter, Marita?"

Marita shook her head. "Nothing. Nothing's the matter. Let's eat, drink and be merry."

"You look like you were going to add 'For tomorrow we die'," Miguel observed.

Marita went to fetch the glasses from the kitchen, where her mother was flipping the last grilled cheese sandwich.

"Fancy glasses?" Mrs. Gordon asked, looking up.

"They're for champagne."

Now Mrs. Gordon's eyebrows shot up. "Champagne! Are we going to hear some special news?"

"No, Mom," Marita hurried to explain. "Miguel thought it was a special occasion because he was meeting you and Dad."

But unfortunately Miguel wasn't reading from the same script, because as soon they were seated around the table, and the champagne had been poured, he rose and raised his glass. "I'd like you to hear some happy news. Marita and I are engaged to be married."

Marita gulped. She racked her brain feverishly for a way to unwind the last sixty seconds but she didn't seem to have any way of doing that. With a forced smile on her face she raised her glass. There went her idea of fudging the engagement. For now she just had to go along with it.

The news immediately set Mrs. Gordon sniffling. "Oh, children, I'm so happy for you," she sobbed and raised her glass. "Here's to you. To your happiness."

Miguel was beaming, grinning from ear to ear. Obviously he wasn't thinking of his mother's looming disapproval which was sure to come when they went to visit Mrs. Cordova in a week.

How on earth could she untangle this snarled ball of yarn?

Marita noticed her father didn't look as jubilant as her mom. He kept looking dubiously at Miguel.

At last it came out. "You look kind of young," he said to Miguel. "Are you sure you know what you're getting into? How to take care of a wife?"

"John!" Mrs. Gordon cried. She was sitting near her husband, close enough to be able to give him a gentle tap on the arm. "What a thing to say."

"Well, I want to be sure he'll be good to our Martha," Mr. Gordon muttered. "Not like that bastard Ron—"

"John," Mrs. Gordon said, frowning angrily. "We don't want to bring up bad memories at this happy time."

"Well, as far as I could see all that lout wanted was a cook and bottle washer. This time I want to make sure Martha's going to be truly happy."

"Mr. Gordon, that's going to be my main focus in life," Miguel said firmly.

Marita's heart gave a painful jolt. How could she ever tell him it wasn't going to happen?

"Besides, my age has nothing to do with it," Miguel continued, and Marita saw how he looked her dad straight in the eye. "I love your daughter with all my heart."

At his words Mr. and Mrs. Gordon both smiled and Marita knew Miguel had pushed the right buttons.

For a few moments they sipped the champagne silently and then Mr. Gordon coughed and began again. "I guess maybe you've noticed, Miguel, I'm quite a bit older than Ruth, here."

Miguel nodded. "Yes, I understand you have an age difference."

Marita had already told Miguel her mom was only sixty-five, but did Dad feel it necessary to bring that up now? Of course! It had to do with the age difference between her and Miguel.

"When I started to court Ruth she was turning twenty. I was pushing fifty. Like Martha is now."

"Geesh, Dad, nice way to put it," Marita objected. "Make me sound even older than I am."

"Well, it's the truth. You can imagine what people were saying about us."

Marita picked at a string on the lace table cloth. "But at least they weren't calling you a cougar." It hurt to say the word aloud.

"No, they weren't, but there's plenty of unkind names for men who marry women a lot younger than themselves. I'm sure you've heard a few of them."

"There's stigma in any relationship that people consider inappropriate age-wise," Mrs. Gordon said and took her husband's hand.

"And there's a good reason for that" Mr. Gordon went on. "Like health considerations. Look at me. I've been in a wheelchair for over ten years. Ruth here's had to look after me all this time." His eyes misted and he turned to look at his wife. "Now if she'd married some younger fellow—"

"I could be doing the very same thing," Mrs. Gordon said firmly. "We have no way of knowing what happens in life. Young men get sick, too. And it could just as well have been me in a wheel chair with some other condition. I mean, look at Marlene." She turned to

Marita and Miguel. "A friend of ours from the church. She got MS when she was in her thirties." She gave her husband's ear a tweak. "So, John, you stop talking like that, right now. And as far as age is concerned, it's all relative. Some people at forty feel like they're past their prime. Others are chipper at eighty. It's all in the mind, as far as I'm concerned. And even though John had that stroke, he's still a force to be reckoned with." She leaned over and gave her husband a resounding kiss right on the mouth.

"Your mother is one helluva woman," Mr. Gordon chuckled and stroked his wife's hair lovingly.

Miguel grinned at Mr. and Mrs. Gordon who continued to gaze tenderly at each other. His parents had never been this open about showing their love. This explained why Marita was so uninhibited when it came to expressing her feelings for him.

"I'm going for my afternoon nap," Mr. Gordon announced. "Don't you praise my virtues too much, Ruth, when I'm not here to defend myself." He laughed at his own joke and wheeled himself out of the room.

Later in the afternoon, Miguel sat at the kitchen table with Marita and Mrs. Gordon. This comfortable home was so different from his own, more formal house. Tea was brewing and a plate of homemade cookies sat on the table. He sighed deeply and sat back, crossing his arms across his chest. He couldn't have felt more at ease. He had immediately liked the cherubic Mrs. Gordon, whose quick movements reminded him of a plump little chickadee.

"This is how our home will be, too, Marita," he said "Warm and comfortable. And loving."

It disturbed him when there was no affirming reply from Marita. Instead she ventured on a totally different subject.

"Mom, I want you and Dad to think about moving to Toronto to live closer to me," she said. "I want to be able to help you more. There's some nice seniors' homes not far from where I live."

Senior homes? Miguel frowned. When he'd just talked about their own future home. It was as though she were avoiding his comment. But why?

"Dear, we've gone over this already. Your dad won't move from here, and that's that." Mrs. Gordon got up to pour the tea.

"Marita and I haven't discussed yet where we'll live when we get married," Miguel put in, hoping to bring the conversation back to his topic. "But, Mrs. Gordon, I want to assure you that you'll get all the help you need, whenever you're ready to move."

He was looking forward to frequent visits to this house, in which he felt the same warmth and love as when Marita was near him.

"I'd be very happy if you would call me Mom," Mrs. Gordon said and offered him the plate of cookies. "Baked them this morning. If you feel comfortable saying that, of course. If not, Ruth will be nice. Mrs. Gordon sounds way too formal."

"I'd be honoured to call you Mom," Miguel said and received a big kiss on his cheek as a reward.

"Boy, you really know how to push all the right buttons, Miguel," Marita said with a short laugh, which somehow sounded strained. Something was up, and he had no idea what it was.

"I mean every word," Miguel said and leaned over to pass Mrs. Gordon's kiss to Marita. "Your family is very easy to love. Just like you are, my darling."

Chapter Eleven

Marita tried to stop the queasy heaves in her stomach as they neared Miguel's home in the town of Kleinberg, just outside the city. She must not be frightened of Mrs. Cordova. She must not! It didn't help. Mrs. Cordova was an unknown, scary entity.

She could see Miguel was excited as a little boy, in anticipation of how surprised his mother would be at the news of their engagement. God, what a tangled web this was! And Marita had no idea how to extricate herself from it. But she was pretty sure the announcement wouldn't be met with celebratory glasses of champagne. Poor Miguel. Men simply didn't get it. He might brush off the idea of no children as a non-issue, but grandchildren were important to older women. Marita could anticipate his shock when his mother would not share his joy with the engagement.

All week long Marita had tried to find an occasion to tell Miguel their engagement was off, but whenever they met he was so happy and enthusiastic about their future, she couldn't bring herself to say anything. It would have been too cruel. But would it be any less cruel to break it to him later? There was no way of avoiding the final outcome, and Marita knew she was only being a procrastinating coward.

Maybe today the whole issue would just naturally blow apart with no effort on her part. Ka-boom! Thanks to Mrs. Cordova.

Finally Miguel pulled into the circular driveway. This was it, then. Marita looked up at the three-storey century house that was beautifully maintained, with the white trim around the windows, doors and eaves-troughs meticulously painted. Even the tall, old trees in front of the house looked professionally pruned, Marita noted, unlike the unruly maples on her parents' street.

Angela met them at the door. "Hi Miguel. Welcome, Marita," she said, smiling, and kissed them both. "I'm so happy Miguel finally brought you to visit us. Mother has been looking forward to this so much."

Yeah? Really? Marita didn't want to be negative but couldn't help doubting Angela's words.

Angela led them into the bowels of the house and into what Marita thought looked like something that might be called the drawing room. There she finally came face to face with Mrs. Cordova. The woman looked every bit the way Marita had always imagined an elderly Spanish señora would. Agelessly beautiful, her graying hair carefully coiffed, she stood up and came toward Marita, with her fragile but elegant hand extended.

"Welcome, my dear," the lady said with a smile. "I'm so happy to meet you at last. Miguel has been telling us about you for months and months."

She waved them toward comfortable couches and armchairs scattered around the room. Miguel sat down on a love seat but before Marita had a chance to plant her bottom beside him, Mrs. Cordova sat next to him. Okay, no problem.

Marita smiled. "Surely he's not talked about me for months. We haven't known each other that long."

"I'm sure it's months." The lady frowned and turned to her son. "Miguel?"

"Well, I guess I may have mentioned your name last spring when I met you at the art class." Miguel looked a bit sheepish. "That's what mother is probably remembering."

Wow! Would Miguel have talked about her way back in the spring? It was very satisfying to think that while she'd been secretly drooling over him, he'd been interested enough in her to mention her to his mother.

"Yes. He mentioned you last spring." Mrs. Cordova said. "But it's been this fall that your name has come up more and more often. So I wanted to meet the lady who has bewitched my only son." She smiled at Marita while lovingly stroking Miguel's arm beside her.

To Marita the gesture seemed rather possessive. Or were her own possessive feelings about Miguel bubbling to the surface? Mother versus daughter-in-law battles starting already, even before they had assumed the roles.

What was she thinking? They never would hold those titles!

Miguel looked embarrassed. "Mother, please." He turned to Marita. "She's behaving like one of those Old World Spanish mothers, even though she was born right here, in this very house."

Mrs. Cordova gave Miguel a reprimanding tap on the arm. The gesture, Marita thought, would have been perfect if she'd been holding a fan.

"You naughty boy, how dare you call me an Old

World mother." But the words were accompanied by an indulgent smile. She turned to Marita. "I'm very modern, even if I live in this old house. I don't know if Miguel has told you, but his grandparents bought it when they came from Spain at the end of the thirties. After Miguel's father and I were married we decided to live here with them, since they were both getting old. We took care of abuela and abuelo until each of them passed away."

"That was very kind of you," Marita said and tried to adjust her preconceived notions of the lady. She wasn't scary. She was elegant and beautiful, and kind and loving to her family.

"It is what a family does," the lady remarked. "Looks after one another. Yes?"

The questioning look Mrs. Cordova gave her made Marita feel as if there was some doubt about her own family not being equally caring.

"I assume your parents are quite aged. Are they still alive?" the lady asked.

The question was innocent enough, but Marita felt like there was something not quite right about it. Did the lady consider Marita so old her parents might no longer be living? Or was that her own age-issue surfacing again?

"Oh, yes," Marita replied brightly. "My mom is in great shape, but my dad hasn't been all that well after his stroke, I'm afraid."

"Yes, these things happen as people age."

That so? Marita refused to think unkindly about the remark and instead got up to look out at the gardens, which were visible through the wide bay windows. "Lovely gardens, Mrs. Cordova."

"Thank you. I love them. They are a lot of work but

the results are worth every ounce of effort. Do you garden, my dear?"

The question made Marita feel that if she confessed to not having a garden, she would lose some Brownie points in Mrs. Cordova's eyes.

"Marita lives in an apartment," Miguel hurried to explain.

Which didn't exactly help the situation.

"But my parents have a garden," Marita said in an effort to raise her status by at least a tiny bit.

Why was she feeling more and more like a persona non grata? It had to be because she wanted so much to be liked by Miguel's mother and was being overly sensitive to non-existent nuances in the lady's words.

Or was it because, while the lady asked her innocent questions, her dark eyes were sharp?

"We'll go into the solarium, shall we?" Mrs. Cordova suggested and obediently everyone rose. "The flowers there are blooming beautifully. It's too cold to go out today, even though the sun is shining, but we'll have lunch in there and be able to view the garden. I think I'll put on my shawl. The solarium is not that well insulated and I know I'll feel the chill."

Marita hung back and whispered to Angela, "Where can I find the bathroom?"

"I'll take you there," Angela said. "These old houses can be a bit convoluted and confusing."

Angela led the way down a hall and around a few corners to a lovely old-fashioned bathroom. When Marita came out she looked around, trying to think where the solarium could be. She had no idea which direction she should go, and for a while she wandered around, down one hallway and up another. When she rounded another corner, she came to a stop when she heard Miguel speaking in a hushed but angry voice.

"Mother, you have no right to say such things about her."

Marita froze. She couldn't have moved if she'd wanted to.

"Miguel, you know very well she's too old for you," Mrs. Cordova said, obviously not even trying to speak quietly. "You're a beautiful, talented young man with your whole life ahead of you, and I have such hopes for you. Why would you choose to marry a divorced woman who is well on her way to fifty?"

"Because I love her. I have asked her to be my wife and she has said yes."

"Of course she would say yes," Mrs. Cordova cried. "Any woman in her right mind would say yes to a wonderful man like you. Especially a woman whose chances of getting a husband are getting very slim. Can you not understand, Miguel, that she really is too old for you."

"Mother, please don't talk like that," Miguel hissed angrily. "Marita and I were going to tell you together about our engagement, but now I've told you and spoiled the surprise. And you're certainly spoiling the whole thing for me. How can I now pretend in front of her that things are all right and you're happy for us?" Miguel's voice changed to pleading. "Mother, please try to understand that the age difference means nothing to me. She's a wonderful person. I love her and she loves me. That's all that counts."

Marita trembled. She couldn't tell if it was from fury or from shock. She wanted to step forward and show herself before she heard any more awful words, but she remained glued to the oriental carpet.

"She's divorced. The Catholic church won't even

marry you." Mrs. Cordova's voice was getting louder.

"Hush, Mother."

Although she was shaken to the core, Marita could understand the lady's growing desperation at her son's obvious stupidity. But at Mrs. Cordova's next words, Marita's heart sank. It was the clincher she'd been expecting.

"And she is too old to provide you with a child, Miguel. Think of that. You're my only son and I've always counted on you to carry on the Cordova name. Maybe it makes no difference to you now, but eventually you will want children. Everyone does. What will you do then, when it is too late?"

"I'm not marrying Marita to have children. I'm marrying her because I love her and I want to be with her forever."

"But what about me?" Mrs. Cordova's voice rose in pitch and then broke.

Was it for real or for effect? Marita felt guilty for even having such unkind thoughts. Then she heard the sobbing.

"I have always looked forward to having grandchildren."

Mrs. Cordova was right. Marita was too old to have children. And it was possible the fall and the miscarriage had ruined her chances to have children even had she been younger.

She leaned back against the wall and forced herself to breathe calmly. It did no good to have a breakdown over this. Facts were facts. Period.

She squared her shoulders, turned around, and resumed her search of the solarium. As she went around another corner she bumped into Angela who was carrying a tray of tiny sandwiches.

"How do I get to the solarium? I seem to be lost."

Angela nodded. "Easy to do. You go down this hall and at the end turn left and you're there. I'll be there in a minute."

Miguel was just helping his mother get settled into a rattan chair when Marita breezed into the solarium with a wide smile on her face. The room was almost filled with a variety of potted plants that had been brought in from the garden for the winter. Although it was November, outside a few yellow, red and pink roses were still in bloom, the colours showing beautifully against the neatly trimmed evergreen hedges.

"This is so lovely," Marita caroled brightly. "What a great idea to have lunch here." Was this cheerful enough?

The act obviously was believable, because Mrs. Cordova smiled back at her.

Yeah, the smile of an old crocodile. But there was no reason to be bitter. After all, the lady had only voiced her own thoughts on irrefutable facts of nature. They applied to all women past a certain age, so no use fighting it.

"Not too many days like this left, I'm afraid," Mrs. Cordova said. "I thought we would take advantage of it."

Another fact of nature—autumn had arrived. No use fighting that, either.

"Ah, yes. Autumn has irrevocably arrived, hasn't it." Marita sat down and crossed her ankles demurely. "Just like in life, after summer comes autumn." Should she smear it thicker? "Too bad we humans only get one kick at the can when we're young. Unlike the flowers, which bloom anew each spring." She shook her head mournfully and pursed her lips.

Miguel turned to look at her and raised one questioning eyebrow, but said nothing.

After lunch Mrs. Cordova rose and, with an elegant swirl of her shawl, turned to Marita. "Dear, I'd like to show you something in the library."

Goodness, the house even had a library? What didn't this house have? Maybe there was even a torture chamber in the basement!

"Of course." Obediently Marita put down her empty teacup and rose.

Miguel began to get up, too, but with an imperious wave of her hand his mother indicated for him to remain seated.

"I wish to chat only with Marita," Mrs. Cordova said. "Girl talk," she added with a coy little smile.

Yeah, like a cat inviting a mouse to join her for some cheese.

"Mother, I don't think—" Miguel began.

"Miguel," his mother cut him off. "We don't need you, dear."

Marita saw the frown on Miguel's face as he settled down again. She was pretty sure he suspected what the "girl talk" would be about. Fortifying herself with a deep breath she followed the lady out of the room.

They entered the library and despite her fluttering heart, Marita couldn't help being impressed as she looked around her. The room was panelled with dark wood and the walls were covered with shelves of impressive-looking books. Above a massive natural stone fireplace was a wall of family photos.

"Cordovas," the lady said as her arm swept across the wall.

There were daguerreotypes, old sepia-coloured

wedding photos in dark oval frames, and a variety of more modern portraits. Among the most recent ones were formal coloured ones of Miguel and Angela as toddlers.

"We are an old and proud family."

"Yes, I get that impression," Marita said. "Old and proud."

"I would be very disappointed if this Cordova family branch were to disappear with Miguel."

Marita nodded and pursed her lips in total agreement. "Yes, I can see why. There's still a lot of wall-space to cover."

"Miguel must have a son to carry on the Cordova name." The statement left no room for argument.

"Hey, isn't that like royalty?" Marita exclaimed guilelessly. "Though I think in many royal families today even girls are allowed to inherit the crown."

Mrs. Cordova looked at her askance. "We prefer the name to be carried on with a male heir."

Marita nodded. "Yeah, I guess some traditions die hard. Of course, if Miguel only had daughters, he could always adopt a son."

"Oh, no," Mrs. Cordova exclaimed. "That would never do. It's the blood that is important."

"Blood. Yes, of course. But maybe the kid could have a transfusion?" That was about as far as she was able to carry on with this farce because Mrs. Cordova was looking at her like she was beginning to see through Marita's dumb act.

"What I am saying, Marita," Mrs. Cordova elucidated, and her voice was as cold as her eyes, "is that it is not a good idea for you and Miguel to marry."

"Marry?" Marita felt like she was bleeding inside. Or was it her happiness draining out of her? Somehow she was able to laugh with surprise that almost sounded real. "Oh, my goodness, I have never even considered marriage." The important thing now was to keep from breaking down in front of this woman.

"Oh?" Hope was dawning in the lady's eyes. "But Miguel made me to understand you two were engaged."

Marita laughed again. "He's such a silly boy. He thinks in order for us to have . . . you know, a sexual relationship, we should at least be engaged. He's such a good lad. But that's all there is to it." How much more nonsense could she spew out before her lunch started to follow?

"Well, I am very relieved to hear that," Mrs. Cordova said and this time her smile seemed genuine. "Why don't we go and join the others in the solarium."

Marita's heart was ready to burst. "You go ahead. I'll just visit the little girls' room," she simpered. Yes, and throw up in there. "Oh, and by the way," she threw over her shoulder as she went down the hall. "I am a Catholic." But she wasn't sure the lady heard.

She stood in the bathroom, taking in huge gulps of air, telling herself everything was evolving just the way it should be. She had never entertained the thought of marrying Miguel. She had expected him to leave her as soon as he found someone more suitable. But it had been easier to keep telling herself this than it was to accept it as the inexorable truth. And hearing it straight from the horse's—Mrs. Cordova's—mouth was excruciatingly hurtful.

Since she and Miguel had begun their relationship, there had always been that faint ray of hope inside her heart which she hadn't been able to squash, and she had fluctuated from hope to denial and back again.

But now it was time to extinguish any residual beams and be brutally honest, even pitiless, toward both herself and Miguel.

Moments later, when she emerged from the washroom, she almost bumped into Miguel who had obviously been looking for her.

"Marita, I want to talk to you." Before she had a chance to object he took her firmly by the arm.

"Goodness. Everyone wants to talk to me this afternoon," Marita exclaimed as Miguel steered her down the hall. "I swear, I've never been so popular in my entire life."

Anger roiled inside him as Miguel led her into the kitchen and closed the heavy wooden door behind them.

He stood her against the large granite island in the middle of the kitchen and positioned himself in front of her. "What is going on, Marita?"

"Going on? Whatever do you mean?"

Her eyes were far too big, far too innocent-looking, and he wasn't taken in by her obvious act.

"This sure is an impressive kitchen," she said. "Is this what you wanted to show me?"

"Stop this nonsense, Marita. You're acting like an idiot. All this nonsense about autumn there in the solarium."

"What's wrong with that? I was simply making small talk about the seasons." She avoided his eyes.

He took her by the shoulders and forced her to look directly at him. "I wish it had been small talk, but it wasn't. You overheard mother and me talking in the hall, didn't you?"

Her body was stiff and unresponsive under his hands and that told him everything. Damn right she'd heard.

Marita looked at him for a long moment, as if weighing whether to admit the truth or not. "Okay," she said at last. "I did overhear you, and your mother is absolutely right. I am too old for you. I wasn't going to talk to you about it while we're here, because—" she swallowed. "Because I was afraid I might start to cry. But now that you brought it up—"

Her eyes filled and she twisted out of his embrace. "See?" she cried roughly. "I was afraid of this." She rushed to the counter, ripped a paper towel off the roll and dabbed her eyes. "Did you have to bring it up now?" she shouted. "Couldn't you at least have waited till we were in the car, for God's sake? Let me keep some of my pride?"

Miguel felt her pain in his chest. He knew her heart had already been broken, crushed by his mother's words. How horrible it must have been for Marita to have to listen to all that. He tried to take her in his arms, but she turned away angrily.

"Leave me alone."

"I'm sorry you overheard us," he said. How the hell was he going to make her listen to reason? How could he make her see his mother's words meant nothing to him. The only thing he couldn't stand was losing her.

"Oh, you're sorry because I heard? You'd rather I had carried on, totally ignorant of the fact that I was not wanted by the family Cordova? That is not nice."

"No, of course not. I didn't mean it that way. Marita, you're upset. We'll talk about this later."

"Me? Upset?" Marita's laugh turned into a hiccup. "Why should I be upset because your mother said something very sensible and very true? I'm glad I overheard you."

"Darling—" Miguel tried to break in, to prevent her from saying what he knew was coming next.

"Do not darling me, Miguel Cordova," Marita said firmly. "There will be no more darlinging between us." She finished dabbing her eyes with the paper towel. "Where's the garbage? Or do you recycle these?"

Angrily Miguel grabbed the towel from her hand. "Don't play games with me, young lady." He was not going to lose her again, not after just having got her back. Not after almost winning her for his wife.

Marita guffawed loudly as she turned to walk away. "Young lady? Such an inappropriate choice of words. Your mother would never agree." She pushed the heavy kitchen door open with both hands. "And I'll thank you not to bring up the subject of the engagement. Luckily you never got around to buying a ring, because the deal is D.O.A."

"Damn it all, Marita! Please—" He reached for her, but she slipped through the door, away from him.

"Don't worry. I'll make sure I don't behave like an idiot in front of your mother," she said over her shoulder."

There was little talk as they drove back to the city a few hours later. At first Miguel tried to make some light conversation, but the stony wall of silence greeting his attempts soon made him give up kicking the dead horse. He'd told her their age-difference meant nothing to him. He'd told her he didn't care about having kids. He'd told her he loved her. What else could he say to convince her?

"Let me out at the door," Marita said stonily when they got near her apartment. "I don't want you to come up."

But Miguel didn't stop the car until he'd found a parking spot. He got out with her. "I'm coming up."

"I don't want you to."

"Well, I'm coming anyway." He held the glass front door open for her and followed her as she walked stiffly toward the elevator.

At her door she dug the keys out of her purse and unlocked the door. "You're not coming in, Miguel." Her voice was quiet and determined. "I don't want to talk to you."

But Miguel wanted to ignore her words and push his way in. He wanted to hold her and not let her go until she understood how ridiculous this whole thing was. Until she understood that the issue of age and children had nothing to do with their love for each other.

"Look, Marita, I—" he began, but she opened the door and slipped in without looking at him.

"Good-bye, Miguel."

The words sounded ominously final. And as he heard the click of the door lock, he had a terrible premonition she was locking him out of her life forever.

He pressed his forehead against the door. "Marita," he whispered. He was sure he could hear his heart breaking.

After a while he turned and headed down the hall and instead of waiting for the elevator, he took the steps down. He needed to do something so he wouldn't go back and punch a hole in her door.

He couldn't very well curse his own mother, but he sure wanted to.

Miguel's phone calls to Marita went unanswered. At her work they said she had taken some time off, but offered no other hints as to her whereabouts. And even Lisa wouldn't tell him anything. Marita was lost to him, and he was lost without her. After having found her, he was again going through the same agony. Only this time he had a horrible feeling Marita wasn't going to be coaxed or cajoled into coming back.

He missed her. Missed talking with her. Holding her in his arms. Sharing jokes with her. Missed hearing her low, bubbling laugh. And the feel of her hands caressing him. He even missed the way she would burst into song at the drop of a hat. Without her, all life seemed to be sucked out of his world.

He resented his mother and refused to visit her. It was her words that had made him lose Marita. He knew it would be best if he wasn't anywhere near her, in case his anger made him say something a son should never say to his mother. Something unforgivable.

Only Angela's entreaties finally made him agree to go home for a weekend. But he went reluctantly, and only sat in the library holding an unread book on his lap, not bothering to shave or get out of his dressing gown the whole day.

Finally, as dinner time was nearing, Angela came into the library and stood in front of him. "You're a pleasant lump," she said accusingly. "Could you at least change and come to the table and eat with us?"

"I'm not hungry."

His mother entered, cautiously approaching him. "Miguel," she wheedled, standing behind him, stroking his head. "You have to eat something, dear."

Miguel balled his fingers into fists to prevent himself from brushing her hand away. "Mother," he said tersely, gritting his teeth. "I said I wasn't hungry. I want to be left alone." She needed to leave before he said something rude.

Mrs. Cordova sighed heavily, turned and left. Angela sat near him on a straight-backed antique chair.

"Mother told me about her talk with Marita," she began.

"Yes. She drove Marita away with her cruel words." The bitterness inside him poured out through his voice.

"That may be true, but Mother said Marita told her she had never even thought about marrying you."

"That's a lie!" Miguel exploded. "Marita said she'd marry me. We'd already told her parents we were engaged. When we came here that day we were going to make the announcement to you and Mother."

"But why would Marita tell Mother she had never planned to marry you?"

"Because she overheard Mother say she's too old to have children. She was just trying to preserve her dignity." Miguel clenched his jaw. "Damn that woman!" With each word he hit the arm rest with his fist.

Angela jumped up and quickly clamped a hand over his mouth. "Miguel, you can't say things like that about your own mother."

"I don't care," he muttered although he knew she was right. "Leave me alone and you won't hear me say things like that."

Without a word, Angela turned and left the room, and Miguel sank deeper into the chair. He wanted to curl up and go to sleep and never have to wake up to face another day without Marita.

Chapter Twelve

Marita stood by the bathroom sink, feeling very unwell. At work they knew she was taking some days off, so she didn't have to call and tell them she was suffering from some flu bug or other.

She emerged from the bathroom and plopped down on the couch.

"You better keep away from me because I don't feel well," she said to Lisa. "I think I have a touch of the flu."

"One doesn't have a touch of the flu. One either has the flu or one does not have the flu," Lisa preached like a professor in a medical school. "Maybe you ate something that doesn't agree with you. I'll take your temperature and that should settle the matter."

"It's all right. I don't feel feverish," Marita objected, but soon she was sitting with the thermometer sticking out of her mouth.

After the thermometer beeped, Lisa inspected it. "No temp," she pronounced. "So it must be something you ate."

"You and I had the same thing for dinner last night," Marita said. "And I haven't even had a chance to eat anything this morning. Didn't feel like it." She thought for a while. "In fact, come to think of it, I've felt kind of queasy on several mornings lately and haven't felt much like eating breakfast."

"You haven't felt like eating breakfast? Your favourite meal of the day? That sounds to me like morning sickness." Lisa sounded much too casual to be making such a profound statement.

With a yelp Marita bounced up from the couch. "Morning sickness? I can't have morning sickness. Miguel and I always used protection. Besides, I'm too old for morning sickness."

"In my sex ed. class they always warned us that condoms are not one hundred percent fool-proof."

"Of course I know that, but—" Could it be true? Marita shuddered. "I don't believe it's true in this case."

"Like any calamity, you always think it only happens to someone else," Lisa said very calmly and very annoyingly.

"Oh for God's sake, Lisa, stop preaching," Marita exploded. "I am not pregnant." She made a dash for the bathroom.

After the bout of nausea was over, she looked at herself in the mirror. She looked terrible. White as a sheet. Could it be possible?

She came out of the bathroom. "I'm not up on these pregnancy things," she meekly confessed to Lisa, who was packing her backpack for school. "But I bet you and your girlfriends know the latest technology available. What should I do?"

"Go to the drug store and ask for a pregnancy test," Lisa advised her. "It's really simple to administer and gives you the results in minutes."

Marita eyed her suspiciously. "And how is it you know about these things so intimately? You haven't had to take the test yourself, have you?"

Lisa laughed. "Don't worry. I haven't done anything stupid. But lots of girls use them to check up on missed periods. How are yours?"

"Fine. I've always been a bit irregular. Last month was kind of skimpy, but I had the normal sore breasts, so I can't be pregnant." Marita crossed her fingers mentally. She hoped.

Lisa heaved her backpack over one shoulder and turned to leave. "So go get the test and stop worrying," she said. "Of course the skimpy period could have been implantation bleeding," she said as she opened the door.

"Whoa! Halt!" Marita called to stop her. "What are you talking about? What kind of bleeding?"

"Implantation. Look on the internet and you'll see. I gotta go. Bye!" Lisa closed the door behind her.

Marita shook her head in disbelief. Such a relaxed attitude. Young women sure were different these days. But would Lisa have reacted quite so casually if she, herself, had been in this uncertain situation?

Marita poured herself a cup of coffee and sat down at the kitchen table. Immediately she got up again, dumped the coffee into the sink and rushed to the bathroom.

Returning to the kitchen she decided she would get the pregnancy test and find out for sure what was bugging her. Maybe, if she was lucky, this was only some lethal strain of Ebola.

An hour later Marita sat at the kitchen table again, head in her hands. It wasn't influenza. It wasn't Ebola.

She was pregnant.

Damned untrustworthy condoms! She thought back to the many times she and Miguel had made love and tried to pinpoint the time it could have happened, which was a pointless exercise. The miscarriage had lulled her into thinking her ability to conceive had been compromised, so she'd never even considered the possibility of getting pregnant. Besides, at her age . . . That's what came from being over-confident.

But what was done was done and it was no use trying to stuff the toothpaste back into the tube, so to speak.

So. She was pregnant.

All at once a feeling of pure joy gurgled up inside her. She'd been given another chance to be a mommy! After thinking it would never happen to her, she was pregnant. Marita gently rubbed her belly. It was incredible. There was a treasure hiding inside her. A boundless feeling of elation filled her and with a whoop she began to dance around the room.

"I'm going to be a mommy!" she shrieked and twirled around crazily.

She patted her belly. "Hello, little guy or little gal," she whispered. "Mommy loves you, sweet little embryo. And the whole world will love you when you grow into a sweet darling baby."

She had to get in shape. She had to make sure she was a fit mother who could look after a busy toddler.

When Lisa returned home that afternoon, Marita, wearing her gym tights, was jogging around the apartment.

Lisa's jaw dropped. "What on earth are you doing, Marita?"

"I'm exercising," Marita announced enthusiastically. "I'm going to be a mommy, and I'll have a toddler to chase after, so I have to get in shape."

"Wow!" Lisa exhaled. "So obviously the test came back positive."

Marita stopped, took a few deep breaths and circled her arms. "It did. And I think that is absolutely fantastic!"

Lisa took off her jacket and hung it in the hall closet. Marita grinned as she saw Lisa eyeing her dubiously.

"You think I've flipped?" Marita asked cheerfully, lifting up one knee after the other. "I haven't. I'm ecstatic that I'm going to have a baby after all. For years I thought I could never be a mommy, and now—" She jumped up, clapped her hands and shrieked, "I am!"

Lisa ran up and joined hands with her. Together they danced crazily around the apartment.

"Don't you dare to ever call me old aunt Martha again," Marita puffed when they stopped for a breath.

"I've never called you old," Lisa objected. "It was always you who insisted you were *sooo* ancient."

"That's true. But never again. Old people don't have babies, so obviously I'm not old." Her heart was so full it was almost impossible to contain all the happiness that bubbled inside her.

But Lisa, ever the pragmatist, soon burst the bubble. "How are you going to handle your work and the baby?" she asked.

Reality hit Marita between the eyes. Could she earn enough to support herself and the baby? How would she manage?

Deflated, she collapsed into the armchair. "You're right. I don't know how I'm going to handle my work and the baby." Suddenly her brain felt like a huge ball of fuzzy angora wool and she couldn't seem to find an end to grasp onto.

Lisa went to get her phone. "I'll call Mother. She'll know what to do."

And so, exactly two hours later Rosalyn stormed in through the door like a hurricane. "I cannot believe I heard Lisa correctly on the phone. You're what?" She removed her winter coat and threw it on the back of the armchair.

"You heard her correctly." Marita said. "I'm pregnant."

Rosalyn parked herself at the kitchen table. "I need a cup of coffee," she said with a huge sigh. "I've been zooming down the highway like a race car driver for two hours. Lisa, make us some coffee, honey."

"The smell will make me barf," Marita warned her.

"Tea, then," Rosalyn conceded. "Or better yet, a glass of brandy."

"I don't have any. And I wouldn't drink now, anyway."

"How about camomile tea. Will that agree with you?" Rosalyn asked carefully.

Marita joined her sister at the table. Lisa made the tea and set the table for them before withdrawing into her room.

After she had drunk a few sips, Marita said, "Yes. It seems to be staying down."

"Well, I still don't believe you, Martha," Rosalyn picked up her preaching where she had left off.

"It's Marita. And you can believe me. The test doesn't lie. At least I don't think it does."

Marita knew once Rosalyn got past her disbelief and hand-wringing, she would start to offer some helpful suggestions. She was always only too happy to dispense advice and Marita had learned over the years that more often than not it had turned out to be quite good. Like when Ron's infidelities had come to light and she had been too wounded and too confused to act, Rosalyn had advised her to pack up and leave and move into their home till she found a place of her own. Sisters like that were to be cherished, even if they sometimes came down somewhat heavy.

"I find it incomprehensible how you got yourself knocked up at your age. How come you weren't being more careful? It's not like you're some inexperienced teenager."

Marita winced. Somewhat heavy? Try a sledge hammer. "Condoms break, you know," she said, resolving to stay calm.

It would be nice to get to the helpful part soon. But she knew Rosalyn had to air her feelings before they got there. And Marita probably deserved the lecture.

"There are other ways to protect yourself, you know."

"I know. But right now that's not the issue. The issue is, I'm pregnant."

"So what are you going to do?"

Finally they were getting to the heart of this conversation.

"Actually, I have no idea." Marita took another careful sip of her tea. It didn't ask to come up.

"You haven't thought about what you're going to do? I can't believe I heard you correctly."

"Rosalyn, I assure you there's nothing wrong with your hearing," Marita said patiently. Snapping at her sister would lead them nowhere. "I only found out about this today and I can't seem to think very creatively right now. Probably the shock. I was hoping you'd be able to help me brain-storm and figure something out."

As Marita had hoped, this changed her sister's tone. Rosalyn's voice immediately became very business-like and helpful.

"Well, first of all, does Miguel know? It is Miguel's baby, isn't it?"

Ouch! Marita jumped up from her chair. "Rosalyn!" she shouted. "Of course it is. Whose did you think it was? Certainly not Ron's!"

Rosalyn ignored the outburst. "So have you told him?"

Marita sat down again. "No. And I'm not going to. We've broken up." She almost choked on the next word. "Permanently." Her heart twisted painfully. She took another calming sip of tea. This camomile tea really was good.

"Listen, Martha—"

"Marita. My name is Marita." She could feel the blood pounding at her temples.

"Okay, okay, don't get so upset. I'm sorry. I keep forgetting."

The fact that Rosalyn actually apologised came as a pleasant surprise.

"Okay,then," Marita muttered. "Start remembering."

She listened meekly as Rosalyn dictated a plan of action. It was supposed to be a suggestion, but sounded more like a papal bull. Despite Rosalyn's rather sad lack of diplomacy it was comforting not to have to deal with this alone. Not to have to think at all. Rosalyn was the fixer.

When they were children, Marita had always felt she was ugly and fat, while Rosalyn had been the pretty one. Not to their parents, of course, because they had considered both girls as marvels to behold, but in the schoolyard Marita had always got the short end of the stick.

Which was probably why Rosalyn had always viewed her sister as someone who needed fixing. And Marita knew Rosalyn had done her level best to fix her. Not always kindly, though, especially when they were young. Chanting at Marita with the other kids, "Fatty, fatty, two by four. Can't get through the kitchen door." That had been cruel, but the intent had been to make her stop eating so much. Or at least that's the explanation Rosalyn had given when Marita had asked why she was teasing her.

And now Roslyn was here again, to fix things.

"Eventually you'll have to take mat leave from your job. And if it's not long enough, you may have to quit," Rosalyn said and poured more tea for herself. "You want some?"

"Thanks." Quit? She couldn't quit. How was she supposed to support the baby and herself?

"I can still work for more than half a year," Marita pointed out. But after that? She would need money to live on. Rent, food, maternity clothes. And when the baby came . . . The idea was getting more and more scary as reality poured in.

The thought of Steve as a possible husband flashed briefly through her mind but she immediately dismissed that. Yes, he probably would take care of her and the baby, maybe even learn to love them both, but even for the sake of the baby she couldn't marry someone she didn't love.

Miguel. A sob shook her shoulders. If only things were back the way they had been only a few short weeks ago. They were so happy, looking forward to their wedding. Or at least Miguel was looking forward to it, while she was going along for the ride, waiting for the right moment to jump off the train. With the back of her hand she wiped away the tears.

"You could go home," Rosalyn said quietly. Her voice reflected the empathy Marita always knew was inside her sister. Maybe fairly deep inside, but it was there, nonetheless.

"Home?" Marita pulled some tissues from the box on the table and blew her nose. She stuffed them in her pocket.

"Yes. You know Dad doesn't want to move to a senior home, but with you there, helping out, Mom could concentrate on taking care of him," Rosalyn said with enthusiasm.

What a brilliant idea. "Rosalyn, you're a genius!" Marita cried and came over to give her sister a hug. Rosalyn's idea was simply made for her situation.

"That would solve a lot of problems with one fell swoop," Marita exclaimed. "Maybe I could do some work from there and only drive to Toronto when necessary."

"Yes. And Mom would love to help with the baby and you could help with the household. The baby would give Dad something to look at besides TV and he would be happy following the baby's development." Rosalie enumerated the points, holding up a finger for each item.

"And you wouldn't have to worry about taking care of Mom and Dad as they age," Marita added with a wicked smile. "We'd all benefit."

"Well, yes. That too," Rosalyn admitted ruefully. "I'm too busy to keep driving back and forth to Kingston all the time."

The ultrasound results were in. Marita sat in the doctor's office in an absolute state of shock.

"Doctor, you—you're sure about that?"

"Very sure." Once more the doctor pointed to the two little shapes clearly visible on the monitor. "You can see them for yourself."

"Twins," she repeated as if to reassure herself that her eyesight was still 20/20.

"Yes," the doctor said. "Natural multiple births occur more often to older women."

"I'll be the mommy of twins," Marita repeated, still finding the news difficult to believe.

The doctor laughed. "That's correct."

No wonder she'd been so violently sick the first trimester. She'd been afraid something was wrong with the fetus and her body was trying to get rid of it.

Then the doctor became serious. "Marita, I know you and Miguel are separated, but don't you think you owe it to him to let him know what he has created?"

"His mother hates me," Marita said firmly. "She said I'm too old for him and can't give her—" she stopped. What was she talking about? She could now present the lady with not just one grandchild, but two at once. Surely that should cancel any problems about her age. "A grandchild," she finished and burst into ringing laughter. "She said I was too old to give her a grandchild. Oh my God!"

The doctor's booming laughter joined hers. "Won't you have fun setting her straight."

Marita sobered up. Yes, wouldn't she, though. It would be so easy to make herself acceptable to the lady by showing her the baby bump and saying, "Here are two grandchildren for you, Mother Cordova. Now do I qualify as your daughter-in-law?"

"I'm not going to tell her," she declared firmly.

The laughter died on the doctor's lips. "Marita, what are you saying?"

"I'm not going to tell her because it wouldn't be me who would be welcomed with open arms. It would be the babies."

The doctor shook his head. "There's such a thing as foolish pride, you know. Think of the babies."

But she didn't want to slither into the "old and proud" Cordova family on the coattails of her babies, or their onesies. No way, José. Foolish pride or not, she wasn't going to do it.

Marita rose and extended her hand to the doctor. "Thank you, doctor," she said. "I feel so much better now that I know I'm not going to lose the babies." But then concern furrowed her brow. "Am I?"

The doctor smiled. "We'll take very good care of you and the babies. I'll be referring you to an obstetrician in Kingston who specializes in multiple births and older mothers."

"Thank you." Marita grinned. "But of course I'm not an older mother."

"That's right." The doctor patted her shoulder. "But you'll let Miguel know, won't you?" He opened the door for her. "You promise?"

Marita didn't answer. She walked out of the medical building, her face serious. Let Miguel know? No way, José! She didn't want to marry him just because she was pregnant and could present his mother with an heir. And a spare.

Of course she knew Miguel would marry her, pregnant or not, but she couldn't see herself being in his family, not valued for herself. She was Marita—

witty and vibrant. Not Rosalyn's ugly fat sister. Or Ron's cook and bottle washer. Or Mrs. Cordova's baby machine.

"I can't get a hold of her," Miguel complained to Mika. "Where the hell has she gone?"

He'd made an effort to go to the studio at least on most days. It was better than looking at the half-finished paintings of Marita in his condo and eating his heart out. He missed her so acutely that all his waking hours were filled with her. As were his dreams.

"She's sublet her apartment," he told Mika. "And Lisa has moved somewhere else. Marita won't answer her phone when I call. I bet she has call display and snubs me on purpose."

"I'd say she's making it very clear she doesn't want you to find her," Mika replied helpfully from his side of the studio.

Miguel groaned. "Yeah, but she knows I love her and want to marry her. And I've told her that kids aren't important to me. What more can I do?" He raked a hand through his hair in frustration.

Mika shrugged. "You got me there. As I've said on many occasions, women are capricious. That's why I don't—"

"Yeah, I know, I know." Miguel turned away grimacing. "That's why you don't want one in your life. But one day, when you love someone like I love Marita, you'll be singing a different tune."

"I very much doubt things will ever come to that. I'm inviolable as far as Cupid's arrows are concerned."

"Bully for you," Miguel scoffed. "But your bragging isn't helping my situation any."

For a while the studio was silent as Mika continued

to work on his project and Miguel sat chewing the end of his pencil. He hadn't accomplished anything for days, but coming to the studio was preferable to wandering aimlessly around his condo all day.

How could he continue to exist without Marita?

Finally Mika looked up from his computer. "Angela tells me your mother is totally upset because you don't go there any more."

Miguel shook his head. "I can't go there. After what she did—after the horrible things she said to Marita, I know I couldn't be civil to her. I don't hate her, I don't think, but she drove Marita away, and I know if I saw her I might say something to her I would regret. So it's better I stay away."

The room was silent for a few more minutes, until Miguel banged his fist on his drafting table.

"Damn it all!" he exploded. "I can't go on like—" He shut up when his voice threatened to crack. His stomach hurt, and with a deep sigh he lowered his head into his arms.

"So if you found her, what would you say to her?" Mika asked.

Miguel looked up. In his friend's eyes he saw unexpected sympathy. Maybe Mika wasn't as unfeeling about love as he tried to pretend.

"I haven't planned anything except to tell her again what I've already said to her." Miguel said. "Why do you ask? Have you some ideas that could work?" He didn't even try to hide the desperate hope in his voice. Any suggestion would be better than none.

"Well, if it was my girl, I'd tell her this situation is simply unacceptable and she needs to come back."

Miguel's laughter rang hollow. "Thanks, but you think Marita would meekly obey me and come home?

You don't know my Marita."

"All women want a masterful man who lays down the law," Mika insisted. "They want a caveman who drags them home by the hair."

Miguel grimaced. "Great. If I ever find her I'll grab her by the hair and drag her into my condo like some Neanderthal," he said. "But since this is the first suggestion you've made, I won't shoot it down, although I can't say it sounds very helpful. Amusing, yes. But not helpful."

He knew even if he found her, Marita would never come back. Not even if he dragged her to his cave. Not after what his mother had said.

He stifled a moan. What his mother had said was all so unimportant. So trivial. Who cared about the continuity of the Cordova name? Such utter nonsense. The only thing that mattered in this life was the love he and Marita had for each other. How could he make Marita understand this?

"But maybe you should go and see your mother," Mika said. "Angela sounded very serious when she said the lady's so upset she's almost tearing out her hair." He clicked his mouse and woke up his screen. "And now please let me concentrate."

Chapter Thirteen

"Miguel, my dear son, I have been so wrong," Mrs. Cordova said. She stood behind the deep armchair where Miguel had sat slumped all morning. He could feel her hand tremble as it rested on his shoulder.

He'd come home to spend the weekend, but still couldn't face his mother, nor talk to her. And even though in this house there were no paintings of Marita to drive him crazy, it was no better. Mika had suggested he should put the paintings away out of sight, but he couldn't. That would have been like pushing her from his life forever. And he couldn't help it if he still kept hoping. Hoping that he would find her, or that she would come back.

"Miguel, did you hear me? I said I have been wrong," his mother said again.

"I heard you. What have you done now?" The question was rude but he didn't care. Why didn't she get the message that he did not want to talk to her?

There was a sob behind him. "I drove Marita away with my unkind words."

Miguel turned around in the chair and looked her straight in the eye. "Yes, you did," he said coldly and turned his back on her again.

She came around to stand beside him. "I'm so sorry, Miguel. I didn't realize you loved her so much."

Miguel looked up. He had never seen his mother like this. She was wringing her thin hands and tears were streaming down her cheeks. No matter what the situation, his Mother had always behaved like a proud lady, at least in front of him. But even this unusual show failed to gain his sympathy.

"I told you I wanted to marry her," he said. "Did you think I'd want to marry a woman I didn't love? I love Marita with all my heart. She's my whole world. My everything." His voice cracked in spite of himself.

"I can't blame you if you hate me." His mother, also, choked on her words.

Miguel sighed. "Mother, I don't hate you. But I don't understand how you could have done it." He turned his head away to watch the TV screen that wasn't even turned on. He couldn't stand looking at her, weeping there, while he was bleeding inside.

"It is breaking my heart to see you like this," his mother went on. Her voice broke into sobs. "You aren't eating. You are always so sad."

Her sobs failed to move him.

"And you aren't talking to me. I can't take this any more, Miguel."

"Well, you brought it on yourself, Mother. How did you expect I would react? I miss her so much I hurt inside."

She reached down and gripped his hand tightly with her fingers. "Please find her and bring her here so I can apologize to her. Please, Miguel."

Surprised, Miguel turned to look at her. "You mean that? You'd welcome her as your daughter-in-law even though you'll never get your grandchild? So it's not a deal-breaker for you any more?"

"Yes, Miguel, I will welcome her," she cried. "Your happiness is more important to me than anything in the world. More important than any family name. I see that now. I just want you to be happy, and I know Marita makes you happy."

Miguel stood up. For the first time in weeks he felt a ray of hope inside him. "If only I could convince her of that, maybe she'd come back."

His mother clasped her hands together in front of her. "Please try. I want her to know I am so very, very sorry for my harsh words. If only she can forgive a silly old woman who couldn't see what is truly important in life."

But where could he find her? There was no forwarding address for her at the condo office. Or at least they wouldn't give it to him.

"I don't know where I can get in touch with her," he said. "I've tried everywhere for weeks."

"Surely her parents would know," Mrs. Cordova said. "Do you think maybe they would help you find her if you told them how sorry I am?"

For the first time in months, Miguel hugged his mother and gave her a kiss on the cheek. "Mother, I think that might be just the ticket."

Miguel gave a sigh of relief when at last he pulled his sports car into the Gordon's driveway. There had been an early fall of snow and the drive along the six-lane expressway had been slow and treacherous. Huge eighteen-wheelers had sprayed salty slush on his little vehicle, at times making visibility almost zero.

Marita's parents were his last hope. If they would

help him to locate Marita, he knew that armed with his mother's apology he at least had a chance. He'd come in person, hoping that face to face he would be able to better convince them of his mother's sincerity than on the phone. And if they refused to tell him where she was, he had decided to hire a private detective. He had to find her.

He rang the doorbell, his heart thumping from fear and hope. Would he finally be able to locate her?

He heard footsteps and the door opened.

"Marita!"

She stood before him looking as lovely as ever. Even lovelier, if that was possible. All he could do was stare at her, while a flood of relief and happiness swirled madly inside him.

And she stared back, her eyes wide with surprise. And with unmistakeable love for him.

They belonged together. There was no question in his mind. The joy of seeing her erased all the agony of the last weeks and he knew he would never let her out of his sight again. Ever. Even if he had to resort to Mika's suggested caveman tactics.

When at last he was able to speak, all he could do was croak, "May I come in?" The Neanderthal man was nowhere in sight.

Marita moved aside to let him in, and as he passed close by her, the familiar scent of her filled his nostrils. He stopped and without a word took her in his arms. She melted against him, letting him know how much she'd also missed him.

"Marita, come back to me," he groaned against her hair. "This is crazy. I love you and I know you love me. I can't function without you in my life." The feeling of having her there, against his heart, was almost too wonderful to bear.

"I love you, too, Miguel," Marita said. "But I'm sorry, I can't come." She turned her face away but not before he'd seen her eyes fill with tears.

He took her face in his hands and kissed the tears away. "But you have to come. My mother said I can't go back without you."

Her jaw dropped and she backed out of his arms. "You are joking! You know your mother doesn't want me to come within fifty kilometres of her. Or you either."

Miguel shook his head. "No, that's not true, darling. She specifically told me she wants me to bring you over to see her. She has something she wants to say to you."

Marita looked unmoved. "Like what? The last thing I recall her saying is I'm much too decrepit to join the old and proud Cordova family." He heard the deep sarcasm in the words "old and proud".

"She wants me to tell you she was wrong." Mentally he crossed his fingers, hoping she would be reasonable. "She has recognized the fact that only you can make me happy. That's all she cares about."

Marita frowned. He could see the scepticism on her face and knew it wouldn't be easy to convince her. But considering how deeply his mother had hurt her, it was no wonder.

"She wants to apologize to you. In person," Miguel said, taking her hands in his.

"Apologize?" Marita snorted. "I find that really hard to swallow. An old and proud Cordova would never apologize. I expect she's already got a restraining order against me. And if I go near her I'll be arrested."

"Marita, this is too serious for joking. She said she

wants you to be her daughter-in-law."

"You are kidding! Even without a grandchild?"

"Even without a grandchild."

It took a while for Marita to digest this. Miguel was telling her Mrs. Cordova was now willing to accept her into the family and forego the continuation of the Cordova name. That was an incredibly huge shift in attitude. But was it for real? Deep in her heart, was the lady honestly ready to accept her? Maybe she was only saying this to make her son happy. In time would she grow to resent the woman who had "bewitched" her only son and pushed her infertile self into the family? Only time would tell. But unfortunately there was no time, because soon the surprise Marita was hiding inside her would come to light.

This called for some creative thinking.

"Come in," she said and moved out of Miguel's; arms. "I have to think about this. You must admit it's a bit of a shock."

"Take all the time you want, sweetheart," Miguel said as he stepped into the house he was so fond of. "But I warn you, I'm not leaving till you promise to marry me." He hoped the reception of the Gordons would still be as warm as last time.

"Are you honestly telling me she doesn't care if she gets a grandchild?" Marita repeated.

"That's right. She just wants me to be happy." His grin was almost bashful. "And the only thing that makes me happy is you."

As soon as she saw him, Mrs. Gordon swept him into her arms and gave him a tight hug. "At last!" she exclaimed. "My dear boy, you have no idea how happy I am to see you. I've been telling Marita she has to contact you, but you don't know how stubborn this daughter of ours is."

"Oh, but I do!" Miguel exclaimed. "And I'm still not certain she'll come back with me. She hasn't yet told me she will." He frowned at Marita.

Mrs. Gordon glared at her daughter. "Her father and I will kick her out of the house if she won't leave."

They went into the kitchen and Miguel and Marita sat at the table while Mrs. Gordon prepared tea. Mr. Gordon was sleeping, missing the whole drama.

Marita drank her fruit juice, trying to think, but Miguel was sitting much too close, disturbing her thought process. She had to figure this thing out. The only way she would marry Miguel was if Mrs. Cordova's apology was for real. She was willing to give it a try, but she didn't want to divulge the existence of the twins until she was absolutely certain. She could only hope that before the pregnancy became obvious, she would know if Mrs. Cordova's acceptance of her was genuine or simply a way to make her son happy.

She decided to go for it. "So the only thing that will make you happy is lil'l ole me?" she asked Miguel.

"Yes." His reply was quick and emphatic.

"And nothing else?"

"Absolutely nothing."

"Gee, that's too bad," Marita said, shaking her head.

Miguel frowned. "What do you mean?" Puzzled, he placed his teacup on the saucer.

"It's just that now I don't know what I'm going to do with the twins. Are you sure you don't want them?" She patted her stomach and tried to look rueful, even while her heart was ready to burst into a song.

Miguel stared, shaking his head in utter confusion.

Finally Marita took pity on him and let him in on the secret. "I'm going to have twins," she proclaimed proudly. "I mean, we are going to have twins."

Now Miguel looked totally dazed and for a second Marita though he might faint. He opened and closed his mouth but no words came out.

Laughter bubbled out of her. "Miguel you look like a beached fish. Say something. Anything. Say you can't believe it. Tell me I'm going to be a wonderful mommy. Call me a joker. Anything."

When he had recovered enough to breathe again, Miguel hesitantly reached over to place an unsteady hand on her belly. "Babies?" he whispered. "Honest?"

"Honest," Marita assured him, smiling broadly. "Two of them. You can't feel much yet, but they're there, all right." She stood and pulled him up with her. "Come on. I'll show you their first photos. They're so sweet."

Mrs. Gordon was all smiles and shooed them off. "Go on you two. Go look at your babies."

After they'd inspected the ultra sound images, they sat on the couch in the living room, side by side, holding hands. Marita leaned her head on Miguel's shoulder and he stroked her hair.

Funny how wonderful the day had suddenly turned out to be. Although Marita had continued to exercise and had tried to stay positive, she had often found herself forlornly staring out the window. Only thinking about the babies growing inside her had kept her from plunging into a depression.

But now she laughed at her mother, who had been packing her things in readiness for her to go back with Miguel. And she would go, even though the thought of facing Mrs. Cordova still terrified her.

"You look like a pair of cuddly doves," Mr. Gordon, who'd been awakened from his nap, declared. "Reminds me of when your mother and I used to—"

"Stop right there, John," his wife cried.

"What? I wasn't going to divulge any titillating details, honey," Mr. Gordon protested.

"That's because there are no titillating details to divulge." But Mrs. Gordon was laughing as she said this, and gave her husband a smacking kiss on top of his bald head.

Marita giggled. "Aw, Mom, I'm disappointed. None at all?"

"None that you'll ever hear," her mother retorted.

Marita noticed Miguel was watching this exchange with amused interest. Maybe his parents had never shown their love as openly as hers did. He came from a different world. One she didn't yet know. Or trust.

"It's started to snow again," Mr. Gordon said. He'd pulled the curtain aside and was looking out into the darkening evening. "Coming down pretty heavy, too."

"You two are not driving home in this weather," Mrs. Gordon declared firmly. "Miguel can stay in the guest room and Marita still has her own bedroom down the hall."

"Mom," Marita yowled. "You've got to be kidding!"

"Why should I be kidding? You two aren't married yet." But her eyes twinkled mischievously as she said this.

The arrangement left a lot to be desired. They could choose between the guest room, which had two twin beds separated by a heavy old chest of drawers, or Marita's room with only one twin bed. They chose the guest room.

Dismayed, Miguel looked at the two beds. "After weeks of being without you and missing you like crazy, I can't not sleep beside you," he grumbled.

Marita tried to put a positive spin on the situation.

"Hey, this'll give you a taste of what it's going to be like when I'm close to term, as well as after giving birth. There won't be any hanky-panky then, either."

"I'm not thinking of sex," Miguel said, and almost convinced Marita he wasn't lying through his teeth.

"Oh, sure you're not." But could she deny that was exactly what was uppermost in her mind, too?

"Well, not only of sex," he conceded. "Mostly I want to just hold you in my arms and feel you against me when we sleep."

She sighed. "Yes, that would be wonderful, but—"

"You know what? It's going to be wonderful." Miguel started to toss the bedding off the beds, onto the floor. "We'll pretend we're camping," he said.

After fixing up a cosy bed for them on the floor, he began to strip.

"I've been trying to figure out how this pregnancy came about," Miguel said shrugging off his shirt. "Do you think we could try to re-enact the scene and freshen my memory?"

Marita chuckled. "We could give it a try."

Miguel took her in his arms, but stopped. "Darn it all, I just remembered I don't have any condoms with me. I guess we can't make love after all." But even as he said this, a wicked grin spread on his face.

Marita laughed. "Hey, why don't we just throw caution to the winds and take a chance."

When he began to make love to her Miguel was so full of tenderness, that Marita finally became exasperated. "Are you going to kiss and stroke me all night, or are we ever going to get to the nitty-gritty part?" she demanded.

"But what about the twins? Are they going to be all right?"

"They're tucked safely deep inside me, where even you won't be able to reach them with your mighty weapon," she assured him. "Oh, oh!" She giggled. "I see it's getting even mightier after hearing my compliment."

At last Miguel made love to her. But his passion was tempered with such an ardent desire to please her, she knew without question she really was the most important thing in his life.

Afterward, as they lay sated and happy beside each other on the floor, Marita sighed with satisfaction. "That was a masterful job," she told him. "I was beginning to get worried that during the next few months you'd never make proper love to me."

"I have to get used to the idea there's now three of you."

"There's still only one of me. The other two are temporary visitors and will be gone in a few months."

"Tomorrow we'll go and see Mother and tell her about these visitors," Miguel said. "She's waiting for you anxiously, but won't she simply faint when she hears—"

"Miguel," Marita interrupted. "I don't want your mother to know about the babies. Not for a while. I first want to see if she'll really accept me. I mean for myself, and not because of the twins."

"She will," Miguel said. "I know she will."

"But I want to see it for myself. So let's give it some time. Okay? At least till I start to show."

Miguel raised her chin and kissed her nose. "Darling, whatever you want is fine with me. But I know Mother will love you for yourself. Like I do."

But Marita found it very difficult to believe Mrs. Cordova could change her spots so quickly.

As Miguel parked in the driveway of the Cordova mansion, Marita felt like she was entering the lion's den. Totally unnecessarily Miguel came around to open the car door for her and Marita indulged him for the time being, hoping this over-caring would wear off in a week or two. She also hoped he would succeed in keeping the baby-secret, because she knew it would be difficult, with him being so proud of his "accomplishment".

As they walked up the front steps, Marita swallowed and took a few bracing gulps of the cool, wintry air. Surely it wouldn't be as bad as she anticipated. If what Miguel said was true, Mrs. Cordova would meet her with a nice, red welcoming carpet. Yeah, sure she would.

The lady's words might seem sincere, but Marita remembered how Mrs. Cordova's smile, so welcoming at first, had turned out to be a crocodile's grin. But she also knew she would have to watch herself so she wouldn't put a negative spin on everything Mrs. Cordova said. However, after the way she'd been slapped in the face during the last visit, her guard would definitely be up.

Miguel opened the heavy, wooden front door for her and with a shudder Marita entered. Angela met them with her sweet greeting, which Marita had no trouble interpreting as the real thing.

"I'm so glad Miguel was able to persuade you to come," Angela said. "Mother is waiting in the parlor." She lowered her voice. "She's quite nervous about this."

"Well, it's a good thing I'm not," Marita said with a feeble attempt at bravado. She removed her mittens and displayed her red nails. "See? I haven't quite succeeded chewing my nails down to nothing."

They entered the parlor and Mrs. Cordova rose to greet them. Without giving Miguel so much as a glance, she immediately walked over to Marita, both hands extended. It was as though she wanted to get this difficult part over with as quickly as possible, and Marita was only too happy to comply.

Mrs. Cordova took Marita's hands in a firm grip. The lady's hands were trembling.

"Marita, please let me tell you how very, very sorry I am about my harsh words," Mrs. Cordova began. "Miguel has made me realize you are the most important person in his life, and I am happy to relinquish that place to you. You make him happy, and for this I will always be grateful to you." Tears glistened in her eyes. "Can you find it in your heart to forgive an old woman who let her prejudices blind her to what is important in life? Finding someone to love, who loves you back, is a blessing. It is something we should cherish, and we should never do anything to lose this precious gift."

Marita let the woman speak, suspecting she had rehearsed the words and needed to have her say now, before she lost her courage. Or maybe forgot her lines. That was all right. It was a difficult speech to make and Marita appreciated the fact that she had put so much thought into it. She, herself, had no idea how she would respond, since she hadn't known what to expect.

But when Mrs. Cordova had finished, Marita embraced her warmly and the words came straight from her heart. "Of course I forgive you, Mrs. Cordova. Miguel's happiness is very important to me, too, and if you and I can agree on that, there should be no obstacles to us getting along in the future."

And if this goodwill could be sustained until she began to show, and if she was welcomed as a member of the family, everything would be all right. If not, then . . . what? She would take her big, pregnant belly and go with her original plan of living with her parents.

But then Mrs. Cordova delivered the punch line that set Marita's heart at ease.

"And, Marita, if you and Miguel want to adopt a baby, that will be fine," she said. "I promise I will love the child as my very own grandchild."

Wow! Marita exhaled and gave her future mother-in-law another hug. "That is the nicest thing I have ever heard," she said. At least from Mrs. Cordova. And it spoke volumes about the lady's acceptance of the situation.

The Four Winds Gallery was again filled with people, but this time Marita walked among them holding her head high. Miguel's paintings hung on the walls and even though it was her body that was painted against the curved landscapes, she wasn't worried that she would be identified. The women he had painted had long hair that flowed over their breasts, like the shapes of the tree branches behind them. They lay in discreet poses where the hips and legs melded in with the curvature of the rocks upon which they were resting. It was all so natural and lovely that several of the paintings already sported the red dot to indicate they had found a home.

The guests were of different age-groups, from Miguel's artist friends to elderly, serious buyers. Marita saw several of the young faces from Anita's party, but this time around she greeted them quite differently. No more hiding at the snack table, carrying a vodka on the rocks to fortify herself. Now she held a glass of juice and chatted easily with everyone, sure of her position in Miguel's heart. Inside her the budding secret, of which no one in the room but she and Miguel knew, gave her an extra mental advantage.

Steve was there, of course, and congratulated Miguel on his fine work. He had already purchased one of the paintings and Marita had a difficult time squelching a giggle and holding her tongue. What would Steve say if she told him it was her nude body he would be looking at on his living room wall?

It was Christmas Eve. The living room of the Gordons' house was decorated with garlands and candles. The tree stood in front of the picture window, as it always had since Marita could remember. A fire crackled in the fireplace and all the familiar smells of Christmas filled the little house. Snow was falling gently, covering any gray slush and dirt on the roadsides, and the whole scene was starting to look like a Currier and Ives painting.

Marita's parents had invited Angela and Mrs. Cordova to spend Christmas with them in Kingston and the two now sat in front of the fire, holding glasses of eggnog. Lisa and Rosalyn were in the kitchen helping Mrs. Gordon with the turkey. Although they knew about the babies, Marita had given everyone strict instructions not to say anything.

Mrs. Cordova had brought a dish of nougats and marzipans for dessert. "And Angela made some tapas. They are like appetizers," she'd explained to Mrs. Gordon. "I didn't want Miguel to be without his favourite Christmas foods."

"That's perfect," Mrs. Gordon had replied. "Our star cook, Marita, usually prepares the appetizers, but this year she wasn't here to do them. Thank you so much, Mrs. Cordova."

After dinner they gathered in the living room for the gift exchange. Lisa, wearing a Santa hat, handed out the packages from under the Christmas tree.

When everything had been distributed, Mrs. Cordova reached into her purse and brought out a small gift box wrapped in gold paper. She got up and walked over to Marita.

"This is from me, my dear," she said and Marita could hear her voice quiver.

Filled with curiosity, Marita carefully opened the small package. What could the lady be giving her? It was obviously something very special.

It was! Inside the box was a lovely antique brooch. The colourful gemstones glittered as Marita held it up to the light.

"It is exquisite," she breathed. Nothing in her own family's jewelry boxes had ever held anything quite so breathtakingly beautiful.

"It was a wedding gift from Miguel's great-great-grandfather to his bride," Mrs. Cordova explained. "It was passed on through the generations and given to my mother-in-law when she married. She brought it with her from Spain and I received it from her when I married Miguel's father. Now I want to give it to you, my dear, as token of my love and gratitude for giving my son back to me and for making him the happiest man on earth."

Marita rose and gave Mrs. Cordova a kiss. Her heart sang with happiness. This was much more than she could have expected from the lady. This gift of the family heirloom was the final proof she was genuinely welcomed into the family.

"Thank you, from the bottom of my heart, Mrs. Cordova," Marita whispered.

"Please, I would be so honored if you would call me mother," Mrs. Cordova said, holding Marita's hand. "Would you?"

"I would love to call you mother."

Miguel now rose and dug a tiny square box from his pocket. He walked over to Marita and went down on one knee in front of her. "And I would be honoured if you would call me your husband," he said.

Marita's heart filled with emotion and she wiped a tear from her eye. Everything was so beautiful, including the sparkling diamond ring that glittered in the box.

"I know we are already engaged," he said as he slipped the ring on her finger. "But I wanted to do it properly."

Marita pulled a tissue from her pocket and blew her nose. "I don't know what answer I'm supposed to give at this point. I've already said yes to you once."

"How about saying it again here in front of all these witnesses?" Miguel suggested, getting up. He took her in his arms.

"Yes, yes, and yes," Marita whispered in his ear. "Yes, my darling."

"Okay, are there any more surprise gifts to bring out of hiding?" Lisa asked, "Or can I take off this silly hat that's making my hair all flat?"

"I think I see one more parcel over there in the corner, Santa," Marita said.

Lisa pulled out a large, flat package. "It has your name on it, Mrs. Cordova," she said, smiling broadly as she took it to the lady.

Mrs. Cordova's face registered surprise. "For me? It looks like it might be a calendar," she observed as she began to unwrap it.

But when she had opened it, she stared in confusion at the contents. "What is this? It looks like a negative of some sort."

"It looks to me like an ultrasound," Miguel said helpfully.

"An ultrasound?" Mrs. Cordova peered at the image. "Why on earth would someone give me an ultrasound?"

"Who is it from?" Lisa asked, trying very hard to suppress her giggles.

"I don't know." Mrs. Cordova carefully inspected the gift tag, but still looked confused. "It says, 'Love from the twins'."

"It must be a present from the twins!" Marita exclaimed.

There was a sound of suppressed laughter in the room and Lisa giggled audibly.

"But I'm afraid I don't know any twins. Who are they?" Mrs. Cordova said, frowning.

Marita saw a look of annoyance pass over the lady's face. The poor woman probably thought people were playing a joke on her.

Marita went over and pointed to the two tiny shapes on the ultrasound. "It's the first picture of your two grandchildren," she explained.

Miguel came and outlined the shapes. "See? There's one. And here's the other. Mother, you're going to be an abuela," he said and gave his mother a kiss on the top of her head. "Marita and I are expecting twins."

"Merry Christmas," Marita said. 'Your presents will

arrive in the summer."

"Oh, dear God, dear God," Mrs. Cordova kept repeating, while tears coursed down her face. She made no effort to stop them, and Lisa ran to her rescue with a box of tissues.

The tension in the room lifted and everyone burst into happy chatter. It was as though they had been collectively holding their breath and now were free to laugh and talk again.

"Did you know?" Mrs. Cordova asked Marita's mother.

"Yes, we knew. Marita told us when she came to stay here after she left Miguel. The silly girl."

"It was my fault," Mrs. Cordova said and started to cry again. "I was not kind to her."

Marita's father rolled his wheel chair close to her. "Mrs. Cordova, there'll be no more tears," he said. "It's time to celebrate Christmas and the gift of the babies." Smiling, he patted her knee.

"Except tears of happiness," Mrs. Gordon added and wiped her own eyes.

"One more present!" Lisa yelled over the chatter. "Quiet everyone. One more present for Marita from Santa."

Rosalyn smiled and said, "I hope it fits. Now you don't have to hide your belly with those unzipped jeans and long blouses."

Marita unwrapped the parcel and pulled out a floral maternity top and navy blue maternity pants. "Thank you, Rosalyn. You're right. It'll be a great relief to wear clothes that don't pinch and squeeze."

"I hope those will last for a few weeks, anyway," Rosalyn said. "Who knows how quickly you'll balloon with the twins."

"We better have the wedding soon before I spread too much," Marita said. "I'd like to wear something more stylish than a circus tent at our wedding."

"And Marita and Miguel, after the wedding I would be so happy if you came to live with me in the big house," Mrs. Cordova spoke up, clasping her hands together. "We'll all fit into it very nicely. You can have the upstairs suite and we'll fix up one of the rooms for a nursery. That will be so much fun." She stopped, embarrassed. "I mean if you would like to. Please at least think about it."

"Thank you, Mother," Marita said. "That's very kind of you to offer."

Miguel nodded. "Thanks, Mother. It sounds like a great idea. Marita and I'll discuss it."

Marita saw no trace of tears on anyone's face now. The whole room was glowing with happiness, as brightly as the lights on the Christmas tree.

Epilogue

The June sun shone through the windows of the Cordova solarium. Every flower in the garden seemed to be in bloom at the same time to celebrate the twins' christening. Both babies were dressed in long, lacy gowns, looking like a pair of white lilies.

Marita rearranged some blossoms in a vase, while Angela held Alexander in her arms. Mika, sitting beside her, tried valiantly to rock André to sleep but the baby fussed and squealed despite his best efforts.

"If you bounce him that hard you'll have projectile vomiting right on your fancy godfather suit," Angela warned him.

"Let's trade," Mika said, and carefully they exchanged babies.

Angela laughed as Alexander began to howl the minute Mika took him, while André settled comfortably in her arms.

"Alexander knows I'm not his godfather, and he's crying for Michael to arrive," Mika declared in his defence and passed the baby off to Marita. "This proves it. Kids and I don't mix."

"Someday you'll eat those words, my friend," she warned him.

"Never," Mika swore. "Fatherhood is not even a blink on

my radar screen. And never will be."

"Unless your condoms also fail," Miguel whispered from the side of his mouth. "But you may not be as lucky as I was."

"If you call this luck," Mika countered. "Me, I'm lucky to leave for Finland soon and see all those lovely Finnish ladies. Thanks, pal, for being too busy to travel. Now I get to go off again."

"You're welcome," Miguel said. "Being a dad will be much more fun than traveling."

There was commotion at the door as Michael and Shaylee Merrick arrived. They had returned from Europe only a few weeks previously and had been busy setting up their new household in Toronto.

All the greeting, hugging and kissing caused a pandemonium that set both babies howling.

"Sorry we're late," Shaylee tried to explain over the ruckus. "But Michael got lost."

"Your navigating leaves something to be desired, my dear wife," Michael defended himself.

"Don't worry," Marita said. "We wouldn't have started without Alexander's godparents. Here, you hold your little godson." She handed the baby to Shaylee who immediately began to coo at him.

After the baptismal ceremony Miguel, holding sleeping André in his arms, came to sit beside Marita. With Alexander nodding in the crook of her arm, Marita looked around the solarium where all the people she loved were gathered. Even Steve with his new lady-friend had been invited to the christening.

Only a year ago she had been wondering what to do about her weight and now—

"What a difference a year makes," she mused.

Yes, the sun and the flowers were here to stay.

About Karen Rossi

Karen Rossi (the pen name of Kaarina Brooks) has been a romantic since she was a child. She and her sister had their own "publishing company" and wrote about love-struck princes and princesses.

Today she writes grown-up romances where modern-day "princes and princesses" go through heart-wrenching relationship struggles before reaching their happily ever after.

She now also has a real publishing company, Wisteria Publications. Besides romances, she also publishes kids' books and non-fiction works.

She lives in Southern Ontario with her husband and kitty-cat, Lilly.

www.wisteriapublications.com
brooks.kaarina@gmail.com